Dean
Dean
Dean
Dean

Dean
Dean
Dean
Dean

Flash Fiction by

Jim O'Loughlin

Twelve Winters Press

Published by Twelve Winters Press, a literary publisher.

P. O. Box 414 • Sherman, Illinois 62684-0414 • twelvewinters.com

Dean Dean Dean Dean was first published by Twelve Winters Press in 2017.

Cover and interior page design by TWP Design.

Cover photo by the author.

Author photo copyright © 2016 Carole Fishback.

ISBN
978-0-9895151-2-2

Printed in the United States of America

Acknowledgments

Some stories in this collection have appeared, in slightly different versions, as follows:

"Adventures in Marketing," *La Petite Zine*
"Another Story to Tell," *Pierian Springs*
"The Answer," *Marco Polo*
"A Simple Revelation," *dotlit*
"Celery," *Scraps*
"Choices Made," *Flash Fiction Chronicles*
"Half a Genius," *HA!*
"I'm on Fire," *North American Review*
"The Letter T," *Quick Fiction*
"My Future Career," *Defenestration Magazine*
"The Nativity Set," *Facsimilation Magazine*
"Not Full," *The Quotable*
"A Part of Her," *Write Around the Block*
"Pete," *The Sink*
"Pop Song Carbon Footprints," *McSweeney's Internet Tendency*
"The Real Story, Which You Missed," *The Pedestal Magazine*
"Simultaneous Submission," *The First Line*
"Testimony," *Mocha Memoirs*
"When the Aliens Arrived," *Tales from the Asylum*

Contents

*To Everyone Who Braved the Open Mic at
the Final Thursday Reading Series*

*Special thanks to Wally Hettle,
Jerry Klinkowitz, Rachel Morgan and, always,
Julie Husband*

Dean
Dean
Dean
Dean

Celery

⸻

BEFORE YOU TAKE a bite, pause for a moment and tell yourself that you are in an Edith Wharton novel. It is late nineteenth-century New York, and you are attending a midwinter dinner party. As an invited guest, you are appropriately attired in evening wear and looking forward to a decadent dinner featuring terrapin soup, scalloped oysters with cream, broiled duck, and peach-fed ham. It looks delicious, but it all seems so heavy, and you have been suffering from indigestion lately. You desire nothing more than a crisp apple right now, but they are out of season and you know not to expect any for many months.

But then your attention is drawn to a glass vase in the center of the dinner table. The vase is filled with tall, stalky stems with green leaves at the top. It is an odd-looking bouquet, particularly for such a formal event. Your hostess, who looks surprisingly like Edith Wharton, must sense your confusion, because she approaches and informs you that the vase contains not flowers, but celery, sent all the way from California on one of those new refrigerated rail cars. Can you imagine such a thing?

Your hostess, let's call her Edith, reaches into the vase

and pulls out a stem. Then she brings it up to her mouth and takes a loud bite. You could not be more surprised if she had started chewing on a rose bush.

Of course, you have had celery before, as part of a sauce with fowl. But uncooked like this? It hardly seems civilized. Yet, it would be rude to decline when Edith gestures to the vase, so you pick up a stem and take a nibble. It is crunchy, not wholly unlike an apple, and it seems that it has been months since you have eaten anything that was not boiled to mush.

You take a full bite and chew with gusto, ignoring the celery string that has gotten caught in your teeth. Edith smiles a knowing smile and hands you a napkin, and you suspect she understands more about you than you do about yourself.

And now when you eat celery, a vegetable that is available by the bagful in the supermarket at any time of year, you tell yourself to be this character in an Edith Wharton novel, to imagine celery as a rare, hard food in a world of soft, boiled meats. Approach each bite as a delicacy, as an impossible taste of summer in a long, cold winter.

The Letter T

STEPHANIE SQUINTED at the screen. The letters were fuzzy around the edges, and she thought about getting her reading glasses, but instead she increased the font size to 72 points.

"The quick brown fox jumps over the lazy dog" had never quite looked like that before. Two nude bodies lined up side-by-side, then side-by-side again, like a chorus line—no, more like a gymnastics routine.

It was hard to remember being one of the bodies on her computer screen—was it thirty years ago? But there she was, stretching her arms back to make half a Y and holding her leg horizontally for the H. And what was the name of the model she had been working with, Gretel? She was German or maybe Austrian.

Stephanie heard a sound and spun to see Jerry, her husband, leaning against the doorframe, his arms folded and a grin on his face.

"I'm trying to decide if I should be worried or turned on to find you checking out lesbian porn on the Internet."

It took Stephanie a moment to make sense of what Jerry had said, but then she smiled. She and Jerry hadn't met until the mid-80s. The body on the screen was new to him. She explained that it had been 1973, after all, and it all seemed so artistic at the time, and she wasn't sure if she had even been paid for modeling that day. Nor could she say why, earlier tonight, while she was doing the dishes and lamenting yet another snowstorm piling up outside the window, she had looked toward the microwave on the kitchen counter and saw that the extension cord had coiled up into the shape of a Q. She remembered when she too had coiled up in a Q. On a whim, she googled the photographer's name and discovered that the nude alphabet shoot was now available as a downloadable font.

Jerry stepped closer and stared at the screen.

"It's all caps, huh."

"Yes, and it was hard enough for us to make an upper-case G."

"Well, I don't think I'm in good enough shape anymore to make the X with you. But the N, now that I'd be willing to try."

Stephanie laughed. Of course, to Jerry it would all seem very erotic, but what she remembered was a difficult day's work, arching her back to make the top of the C or holding her legs at a 45-degree angle for her half of the W. They spent a full day in a cold studio going, pose by pose, from A to Z. There was nothing sexy about it.

Except for the letter T. For the T, she and Gretel had faced each other, her left leg between both of Gretel's, their toes pointing straight down. She held the small of Gretel's back with her left arm and extended her right arm straight while Gretel mirrored her. Gretel's head was nestled against her neck, and she thought of words like *Titillating*, *Tryst*, and *Tingling*. She had felt the temptation to just let her body tumble.

Adventures in Marketing

When Karen called, I could always hear the desperation in her voice. "There's a focus group tomorrow. I need college juniors or seniors majoring in math or engineering. Can you do that?"

Karen's job was to find subjects for marketing focus groups. She would cold call people, looking, for example, for men aged 18-35 who used a Gillette razor. If you fit the profile, you would be invited to a focus group. For a couple hours of your time, you would get thirty bucks cash, a ham and cheese sandwich, and you would participate in a discussion over the latest Norelco marketing campaign to steal away Gillette users.

Karen was the friend of a friend of a friend, and, though we never met, I became a "profile filler" for her. Karen only called me when she was having trouble meeting her quota, usually the day before a scheduled focus group. At the time, I was a graduate student taking out loans to cover tuition, so who was I to turn down thirty bucks and a sandwich? "Sure, Karen," I'd say, "Put me down as a senior math major. Call me . . . Brian Taylor?" The next day, I would show up at a converted warehouse with fifty people who really did fit the profile for a focus group designed to help aerospace companies determine how to better recruit new workers.

At the start of these sessions, we would all wolf down sandwiches and sodas before being separated into one of four identical conference rooms with a big oval table and one mirrored wall. A perpetually upbeat group facilitator would explain why we were there and tell us that there might be people behind the mirrored wall observing us. Occasionally there would be a cough from behind the glass, and we would all nervously chuckle about that.

I always aimed to do as little as possible. I didn't want to be memorable, and besides, sometimes I knew almost nothing about the subject we were discussing. But I couldn't help talking anyway. You can thank me, Jeffrey Smyth, drinker of between six and twelve Coors Lights a week, for the fact that we have "Miller Genuine Draft Light" instead of "Miller Lite, Genuine Draft." Despite my vow to keep quiet, I had said, "You can lighten something strong, but if you start with something light, how much better can it ever become?" Our group facilitator really liked that comment and scribbled down a note on a notepad. About a year later, I saw the beer on the shelves.

My most memorable moment was when I was Frank Griffith, regular viewer of "Chronicle," the Boston-area television newsmagazine. We were discussing a segment of the show called "The Byways and Backroads of New England." At the end of every episode, they'd interview some guy who still hammered horseshoes or a couple who owned a country inn with a functioning mill wheel. People loved this bit. "It's my favorite part of the show," a large man with a Red Sox cap had said. "You find out so much about Boston." A woman from the suburbs added, "We're all busy, so it's great to have the show find all these out-of-the-way places you can visit." Our group facilitator that session, a neatly dressed woman with meticulous curly hair, thought these responses were great, and she underlined something she had written on her notepad. "Let me ask a question," she said. "How many of you have ever visited a place that has been featured on 'The Byways and Backroads of New England'?" There was dead silence and a couple embarrassed looks down at the floor. Our group facilitator, in the only dent I ever saw in the armor of perkiness, crossed out her note in disgust. You could see her thinking, "the only thing these people do is drive to the mall."

Another time, I was Sam Martin and I helped to rate local TV news anchors. We would see a brief clip of talking heads reading the news and then be asked if we "liked" each person or not. I knew what was going on. Years of journalism school would come down to a question of grooming. Bad hair, particularly if you were a woman, and your career would come to a halt. That was a tough night.

But the time that broke me was when I was Chris O'Malley, a faithful listener of "HIT98, the station you can play at work," though the first time I heard the station was while driving to the focus group. This session, instead of being put in a conference room, we were herded into a larger room with desks and handed a page of those bubble answer sheets. It felt just like taking an exam. We were told that we would hear six-second excerpts of songs. We were to rate each song on a scale of one to seven, depending not on whether we liked the tune, but on how well we recognized it.

I went in with an agenda. I would do my best to make HIT98 play music I wanted to hear. Seven for the occasional Clash song that slipped through. One for anything by Phil Collins. If I didn't know a song, I rated it a seven anyway, just for the sake of diversity. But after a while my persistence was worn down. Song after song after song. Is a mediocre Eric Clapton tune with a good guitar solo a five or a six? Should all Genesis songs also be ones even if Peter Gabriel did the vocals? And what about that catchy Flock of Seagulls tune I was embarrassed to like? Song after song after song. Dozens, hundreds, one hour, two hours. Finally I cracked and just started filling in patterns on the bubble sheet. 1-2-3-4-5-6-7, 6-5-4-3-2-1.

By the end, my wrist was sore. I took my thirty dollars in an envelope and left in a daze. I drove home in silence, six-second snatches of song circulating through my brain. Su-Su-Sussudio.

The Real Story,
Which You Missed

─────

THE FUNNY THING was that everyone at the Town Council meeting except the reporter for the local newspaper knew that it was all about sex. The reporter was a nice kid, fresh out of college, the eager and earnest type, but he was new in town and so no one was going to talk to him about the biggest scandal we'd ever had. To the reporter, it just seemed like a well-attended meeting with an animated discussion about funding for the new recreation center. He'd be disappointed next week when it was back to zoning variances and budgetary reallocations.

If he had been in town awhile, he would have known how to follow the conversation. When Councilman Smith angrily announced, "Taxpayers' hard-earned dollars are being spent to undermine our community," and half the room applauded in agreement, we all knew he was really talking about his daughter-in-law's affair with Councilwoman Olsen's son.

So everyone listened closely when Councilwoman Olsen spoke up in her son's defense. "I think we've all been victims here to one degree or another. Rather than pointing fingers, I'd like us to focus on the future."

"Is this the kind of future you want?" Councilman Smith sneered. He was shouted down by the pro-Olsen faction in the room, and the mayor had to gavel the meeting to order. The room was warm with tension, and a huge crowd spilled out of the Council chambers into the hallway. Still, the reporter just kept writing on his pad without looking up, without realizing that the town was a cauldron of anger about to overflow. We townspeople eyed each other, wondering who would be the next to betray, looking for signs of weakness or guilt. It seemed the only thing we all could agree on was to blame the architect of the new recreation center.

The architect, a small man who liked to wear bow ties, sat in a folding chair next to the Town Council, looking like a defendant on trial. And most people thought he should have been charged with something. We were convinced that all this was revenge on his part for the Council's veto of the original recreation center budget. But the architect just sat there, playing with his bow tie as if he was slightly bored. He was an easy man to dislike.

The original budget would have covered a new gym, revamped locker rooms, and, crucially, separate rooms for treadmills and free weights, each with their own bank of televisions. But when the budget got cut, the treadmills and free weights were put in one room without televisions. Runners and lifters faced each other across an empty aisle.

What happened next was inevitable. The free weights were used almost exclusively by the athletically inclined male students from the college in town. The treadmills were the domain of the young mothers, running to work off baby weight while their kids played in the childcare room next door. Those two groups stared straight at one another while they huffed and strained, one afternoon after another, sweat glistening their skin and undoubtedly being toweled off in provocative ways. Glances, then words, were exchanged.

Before anyone knew what was going on, it all started to happen. Affairs, divorces, unexpected pregnancies. Wives of ministers, sons of doctors, no one seemed immune. The town was in an uproar, though we only talked about it in private—and, at the Town Council meeting, if you knew how to listen, which the reporter obviously didn't.

He was looking down at his watch during the public comment session, when Joe Andersen spoke. This was the Joe Andersen whose wife unexpectedly left town to "care for a sick relative." The architect had claimed that since the design already had been approved by the Council, he wasn't liable for any "buyer's remorse." Joe screamed that "if it can be built, it can be torn down," and everyone but the reporter knew he wasn't kidding. Joe ran Andersen Demolition & Salvage and he had the equipment to destroy the building, which some feared he was only a few drinks away from attempting. Already, after his wife had left town, Joe had taken Russell Taylor's car and run it through a compactor. Russell had been the star wide receiver at the local college, but when he saw his car crushed into a tiny cube sitting in his driveway, he dropped out of school and left town.

And Joe wasn't the only one with a temper. Twice during the meeting, the Police Chief had to stand and clear his throat, each time running his hand across the leather strap of his gun holster. The message was clear for anyone thinking of accosting the architect, like Joe Andersen seemed to be considering.

Well, the Council ended up approving the money for the renovation. It was too late for separate rooms, and there still wasn't money for the banks of televisions, but the architect signed on to a redesign so that the free weights and treadmills faced away from each other. The Town Council agreed to install a couple picture windows, so that now the boys lifting weights could look out onto the statue of the Virgin Mary at St. Michael's across the way. They also agreed to knock out an interior wall and install a one-way mirror so that the women on the treadmills could look into the childcare room and always have their children in view.

That's the real story, which you missed if you just read the reporter's article, "Council Approves Rec Center Modifications." But maybe it's for the best to just fix the recreation center and move on. By spring, people will be running and lifting like nothing unusual ever happened. Joe Andersen's wife is even back in town. Maybe some stories don't need to be told.

A Part of Her

———

I never felt love before. Jessica liked the sound of that, and she said it out loud. It was something she should have said when Jason broke up with her, just to let him know that, in the end, she didn't really care about him either. It would be a good line to use now, if Jason was home. But as she looked up from the street she saw that Jason's apartment—four floors up, three windows over—was dark. She resented that he wasn't sitting there, alone and feeling miserable.

And then, out of the corner of her eye, she saw him, maybe. The car turned down a side street before she got a good look, but it was the same make and color as Jason's car. She hadn't seen the driver, but there was a woman in the passenger's seat.

But it couldn't be Jason. He couldn't be with someone else so soon. Unless, of course, he'd already been seeing another woman before the break-up. No! He would never have done something as evil as that. Then again, she never thought he would have broken up with her.

The only thing Jessica knew for sure was that she was not going to spend tonight staring at the ceiling, unable to sleep because Jason might have cheated on her. She marched right into Jason's apartment building, glad that she had forgotten to give him back his key. She knocked once on his apartment door, just to make sure no one was home, and let herself in.

Jessica didn't have to be in the cast of *CSI* to read the signs in the apartment. Jason had recently vacuumed and cleaned up all the magazines that were usually strewn across his coffee table. There were two wine glasses in the dishwasher and a strand of blonde hair on the couch. She went through his bedroom but there weren't any signs of a woman having been there. The kitchen garbage can had a bunch of empty frozen dinner boxes, so he was still cooking for himself. It was possible he just had a blind date. One of his friends could have felt sorry for him and set him up.

But then she saw it. His college yearbook was on the living room table. It was open to a page of class photos. And there in the middle of the page, with a perfect smile, was Lynette. Lynette, the ex-girlfriend. Lynette, who was beloved by Jason's friends and family. Lynette, who supposedly broke Jason's heart and made him think he could never love again until Jessica had come along.

Jessica couldn't believe it. She pulled out a chair to sit down and something clattered to the floor. It was a lipstick tube. She picked it up and looked at the label. Strawberry blossom. Strawberry blossom? It was the color of a rotting orange, and she half expected it to smell like strawberries.

How could Jason cheat on her with someone who wore strawberry blossom lipstick? Is that what he thought he wanted? Is that what he thought would make him happy?

Jessica opened the lipstick tube and stared at the pristine white walls of Jason's apartment. She let her hand write what it wanted: "PRICK" in big letters next to Jason's prized signed and framed poster of the 1992-93 Montreal Canadiens. "CHEAT" scrawled next to the flat screen television. Then, in a spot close to the floor, a spot he would only see if he moved the couch, in smaller letters "you will not be happy." Jessica pocketed the now-empty lipstick tube, turned off the lights, and let herself out.

On her drive home, she tapped the lipstick tube on the steering wheel and hummed along to the radio. She was in such a better mood now. It had been nice to be back in Jason's apartment. It felt like a place where she belonged. A part of her still missed him. Maybe she'd text him tomorrow.

Another Story to Tell

IF THERE WERE a movie version of Mitchell's life, there'd be a scene where his mother bops him on the head with a coat hanger. Or there could be this great shot of a sailboat wreck where Mitchell grabbed his brother's arm to save him from drowning but lost his grip. Or maybe there'd be some flashback where you'd see Mitchell as a little boy playing with his favorite sled back when he was happy.

But as much as I tried to think of some story like that about Mitchell, I couldn't come up with one. I'd known Mitchell since we were both kids, and there was no easy way to explain why he turned out the way he did. His family was about the nicest people I knew, and I couldn't think of anything awful that had ever happened to him. But Mitchell turned out to be such a bad guy anyway.

And I mean really bad. Beat-your-girlfriend, steal-from-your-grandmother, get-drunk-and-crash-your-car-into-a-school-bus bad. When Mitchell was out on parole and would come back into the neighborhood, I'd always try to keep my distance. So, I don't know why Mitchell goes and decides I'm his buddy. This last time back, he wants to get together to drink and talk about all the good times we had in high school. Shit, he was only in high school that one year and most of it was in the internal suspension room, but, all right, I humor him. We head down to Sully's and hoist a few, and I listen to him go on about when we broke into the DMV garage and set off the emergency flares and that time we were on shrooms and cruised practically to Canada trying to find a bar that would take our fake IDs. We got busted by the cops both those times, but, you know, I don't bring that up.

Now, I'm checking my watch, wondering if I'll get home in time to catch the end of the news and find out how the Sox did. But Mitchell, he keeps ordering beer after beer, lining up the empties like bowling pins at the end of the bar, and expecting me to get all excited about that Easter Sunday when he mooned a group of nuns.

I guess Mitchell could tell I was losing interest because all of a sudden he shouts, "Hey!" and whips his arm around, knocking the empties off the bar like one of those bowling machines that clears the standing pins. When the bottles shatter on the ground, everyone in the bar shuts up, and Mitchell jacks me up against the wall.

"What the fuck?" Mitchell shouts. "You got nothing to say. It's like you never lived your life."

Mitchell throws me to the ground and I wind up sitting in a pile of glass. By then Sully is making his way over to us with that Louisville Slugger he keeps behind the bar, so Mitchell backs off.

Now, I got bottle shards poking into me, but I figure it's

better to just sit still until Mitchell leaves. And he does, this big smile on his face while everyone stares at him strutting out of the bar. When Mitchell goes, Sully comes over and helps me up. I pull the glass out of my ass, and Sully offers me a drink on the house. But I say, "No thanks. I got to head home."

Sully points his thumb toward the door Mitchell left by. "That kid's got 'early grave' stamped on his forehead. I'd find someone else to drink with," Sully says.

I nod and mumble "yeah, thanks" to Sully, and then I head out too, taking a look first to make sure Mitchell's gone. And he is. It's not Mitchell's way to stick around. He got to walk out of the bar like a cowboy after a gunfight. If he hung out afterward, people would realize that he'd be spending the night in the backseat of his car since his parents wouldn't let him in their house anymore. But now Mitchell's got another story to tell.

Simultaneous Submission

CALVIN HAD ONCE complained that there were not enough poets in the world. That, of course, was before he had started editing a literary magazine. Now that he had been the poetry editor for the *Long Short Review* for almost five years, he had begun to wonder whether some sort of licensing system was needed, like the American Medical Association, only for poets. It would limit the number of people who could write poetry and would put restrictions on how many poems could be written in any given year about dead grandmothers, bad fathers, and waves crashing on beaches. Of course, there would be an immediate moratorium on single tears falling down once-innocent cheekbones.

Reading through the slush pile always put him in a bad mood, but Calvin gained inspiration to trudge through the stacks of paper when he looked over at the pristine shelves where the fiction submissions were kept. Eloise, the new fiction editor, had thrown herself into her work with the kind of gusto and enthusiasm that was only a distant memory to him now. Her side of the room was clear and orderly. His side, by contrast, was bulging with envelopes and littered with sticky notes reminding Calvin of all that he had to do.

So it was more out of a fear of humiliation than desire that Calvin slogged ahead.

We regret that we are unable to use a poem about how a broken heart is a heart attack.

An ode to an apple tree was not quite right for us.

Thanks but no thanks for a piece that seemed not quite to have been written as much as printed by a computer program designed to randomly generate text.

And then he read it. The poem came in a plain envelope with an uninformative "thank you for your consideration" cover letter. But before Calvin was halfway through the poem, he could feel the sweat build on his forehead. By the time he reached the end of the piece, he realized that he was holding his breath and he inhaled deeply. He stood up with the poem clenched in his hands and walked out the door. He ambled for blocks, stopping occasionally to glance at one of the lines of the poem. Each time he re-read a verse, he would feel the need to walk again, then he would stare up at the sky or gaze thoughtfully at his own trembling hands.

He had no idea how long he was gone, but when he came back to the office he was a changed man. He walked over to Eloise and gave her a hug, telling her how much he appreciated and would always appreciate all that she had done for the magazine. Eloise fell back into her chair, and Calvin couldn't tell if she was surprised or just scared of him. He would have to explain himself later, but right now he had to call the writer of the saddest and yet the most hopeful poem he had ever read, a poem he had already begun to commit to memory. He knew he would never forget it and that it would be the most important piece ever published in the *Long Short Review*.

Calvin went back to the cover letter, and fortunately there was a phone number. He punched in the number, and someone picked up on the second ring. Suddenly, Calvin felt nervous. He took a deep breath, asked for the author and, with what he hoped was a nonchalant tone, told the author that *Long Short Review* was interested in publishing the poem.

There was a pause. "What magazine is this?" the voice on the line asked.

"The *Long Short Review*," Calvin repeated, enunciating as clearly as he could.

"Oh, wow, you know, that's too bad. That poem ended up getting published somewhere else. I sent you an email. I submitted it almost a year ago and figured that you weren't interested."

"Interested? Yes, we are. We were." Calvin said, stunned. He hadn't read his email for the magazine in at least a month. He stared down at the paper in his hand. It was almost as if the words were fading from the page.

"Yeah, that's too bad. Wow. You know, I'm working on another poem about my grandmother. She just passed away."

Calvin mumbled his condolences, hung up the phone, and let out a moan. Eloise glanced across the room, a look of concern, and perhaps worry, on her face. He turned away from her and stared at the piles of pages scattered across his desk, covered with what was now only print.

Choices Made

LATER, he would be able to consider all that he had left behind and would never see again: the wedding album, the birth certificates, the kids' favorite toys, even the laptop. In the moment though, with the storm surging and shingles peeling off the roof like masking tape, he only had time to grab what he could on the way out. Still, even as he ran to the car, dripping sweat and bleeding from the gash in his forehead, with the river already up to the wheel wells, he realized that the choices he had just made said something about who he was. In his arms, he held a phone book, the cantaloupe that had just turned ripe, and a gallon of milk. And he had made sure to lock the front door.

Six at Five

YES, you have seen me before. Do you remember my name? No, don't feel bad. It happens all the time. I'm Beth Wilcox. I used to be a news anchor on Channel 6. Of course, I did have longer hair then. Does this sound familiar? *It's time for Six at Five.*

You can call me Betsy. I only went by Beth on the air. I still get recognized all the time though. What's funny is that people I've never met talk to me like an old friend because they used to watch me on TV. I've had people come to me for medical advice or ask if I think they should break up with a boyfriend. I've never quite understood why people do that. I think maybe it's because the news is on after Oprah.

I spent almost three years there at good old Channel 6. You know, it wasn't my choice to leave. Really. *Six at Five* had been number two in the tri-state ratings, but then we dropped to third, and pretty soon the station dropped me. They had to do something like that or the management would have had to blame themselves for slashing the production budget. Have you seen the woman they hired to replace me? You know, the one that looks like a marshmallow whenever she wears white?

Sorry, I guess no one expects me to be bitter about it. That's not Beth. No, Beth is enthusiastic and spunky yet not an airhead. It may have looked natural on the screen, but being Beth was a tough balancing act, going from scowling through the foreign news to mixing it up with the sports guy. She could start to tear up or take a good ribbing, whatever it took. Yeah, Beth had it all together. You want to know something funny? I had been a theater major in college, and I only went into journalism because I thought it would be a more stable career. I've had to move four times in the last ten years.

But that's not the kind of complaining you expect from Beth. Things just bounce off Beth, and she starts in on the next story. But, let me tell you, Beth may move on, but Betsy doesn't forget. Betsy wouldn't care if the whole gang of hypocrites down at Channel 6 got taken hostage by terrorists.

Whew, how many of these have I had? Don't pay any attention to Betsy. She has a way of running on. I'll take you up on that drink you wanted to buy me. Tell me about yourself. I want to hear all about industrial refrigeration in Asia. That just sounds fucking fascinating.

Not Full

———

HIS STOMACH rumbled as he approached the mall and saw the familiar row of fast food signs lined up like dominos. He cruised the strip slowly and was glad to see that it wasn't busy. Everything depended on quick service.

Signaling right, he pulled up to the Wendy's drive thru and ordered a triple bacon cheeseburger, stealing a sniff before rolling the bag up tight. After that he got a milk-shake at Steak 'n Shake, then cut across the road for a Taco Bell tostada and a couple pieces of KFC chicken. Then it was McDonald's for fries, Long John Silver's for hushpup-pies, and a piece of ice cream pie at Burger King. Finally, his passenger seat teeming with bags, he parked beside the abandoned Chinese restaurant and began unwrapping.

The setup was tricky. His car had a big dashboard, but it was hard to position all the food within arm's reach. Soon, with his purchases balanced and a towel from home tied around his neck, he was ready. He wanted everything at once, but he had to be satisfied with an initial taste from each station. He took a big bite of the burger, forced a fist-ful of fries into his mouth, swallowed a hushpuppy whole. He sucked on a straw until his face started to turn red.

Then he got a little carried away. He dipped a chicken thigh into tartar sauce and tore at it with his teeth. He pressed his face into his burger as grease dribbled down his chin. He submerged some fries in the melting ice cream pie and slurped them up. Spinning the tostada in a circle, he nibbled around the edges, then took a huge chomp from the center, breaking it into a dozen pieces that slipped through his hands and onto his lap. Then he scooped up all that was left and pressed it into a ball. Sour cream, ketchup, and chicken skin oozed from between his fingers. He cradled the ball in his hands, raised it carefully, and brought it to his lips, savoring each remaining taste, closing his eyes and chewing slowly.

When he finished, he took a deep breath before opening his eyes. The car looked like it had been ransacked. He was covered in crumbs, and the towel around his neck was torn. Foil wrappers and paper bags were everywhere. And napkins, so many napkins. He had not thought he had undone so many.

He wanted to let the moment linger, but he knew he had to clean up. Soon, he would spend another four hours behind a steering wheel, driving a bus route he knew so well he sometimes drove with his eyes closed, followed by more television this evening. For now though, he felt satisfied, content, and a little sleepy. But not full. No, he would never be full.

Half a Genius

———

TRAVIS IS HALF a genius. The problem is the other half of him is an idiot. He's always got a new scam for making money, and sometimes his plans are freaking brilliant, like when he found old UNICEF boxes and walked around the mall getting people to give him change. Genius, right? But sometimes Travis's ideas are flat out stupid, like the time he tried to turn aftershave into alcohol. The thing is that when Travis pitches me one of his plans, I can never tell at first whether it's a great idea or a disaster.

Take the time with the golf balls. I had just finished my lifeguard class at the pool when Travis ran up to me with a story about a cousin who just got promoted to assistant manager at a driving range. Part of this cousin's new job was to buy golf balls, and he had to get a couple hundred every month, new or used. Travis was all excited, waving his arms and pacing, but I was thinking, whatever, Travis, why's this interesting?

It was as if Travis could read my mind, because he looked me and said, "Remember when we skipped school and hung out behind the country club? Remember the 10th hole, the one with the water hazard? In an hour, fifteen guys must have hacked balls into that pond." I could see where he was going.

"That pond's a mudhole," I said, trying to sound bored. "We can't see anything."

Then, Travis reached into his pocket and pulled out a diving mask and a high-powered, underwater flashlight. He didn't even wait for my question.

"I lifted them over at the mall. I got another set for you."

"Why dive for golf balls," I asked, "when you can swipe stuff like that?"

"Who's going to pay me more than ten bucks for a flashlight?"

Travis had a point. And since I couldn't find a good reason why his plan wouldn't work, I agreed to sneak out to the country club with him that night.

It was a warm summer evening when you would have wanted to go skinny-dipping anyway. We drove to the edge of the country club and quietly walked to the 10th hole. Then we stripped down, put on the dive masks, and hit the water. It really was a mudhole. The flashlight didn't help me much, but once I got to the bottom of the pond, I couldn't believe how many golf balls there were. It was like picking blueberries. I stuffed dozens of balls into my bag before I needed air and had to kick up to the surface. When I flashed my light around, I saw Travis's shiny butt as he dumped a bag of balls onto the shore. He spun around and flipped me off before going back under. I dumped my bag on the green and watched the balls slowly roll toward the cup then break right.

I went back in and kept harvesting golf balls. I must have taken twenty dives before I decided I'd gotten most of the golf balls down there. There were a lot of crappy golfers in this town, but it meant that we stood to cash in.

When I got out of the water, I saw Travis over on the green dragging this huge army surplus bag behind him picking up golf balls. I threw on my clothes and went to help, but by then he had loaded almost all the balls.

"What are you, Aquaman?" Travis whispered. "I stopped diving twenty minutes ago."

I helped collect the rest of balls, and then we both dragged the bag to the car. We could barely get it off the ground and into the trunk.

When we finally drove away, I felt like it was safe to talk. "What a haul!"

Travis smiled. "One more thing. We've got to go to that twenty-four hour laundromat."

Now, I should have stopped him then, but what could go wrong? Besides Travis said we had to clean the golf balls before we could sell him.

The laundromat was off the highway by the Industrial Park. It was the kind of place that looked like it had never been new. Travis and I dragged the bag inside and started shoveling balls into a front loader. They rattled around as we tossed them in.

"Is this going to be loud?" I asked Travis.

"Nah, we're in the middle of nowhere. Besides, we're

only going to wash them for a couple minutes."

It took us a while to figure out how to work the washing machine, since neither of us had ever used one before, but eventually Travis slammed the door shut and popped in some quarters.

Then we heard a sound like no other, a combination of fireworks and a machine gun. Through the glass window in the front of the washer, I could see golf balls bouncing around like microwaved popcorn.

"Turn it off!" I yelled over the noise.

Travis twisted some knobs but it didn't do anything.

"Someone's going to call the cops!" I screamed.

Travis spun the knobs again, but nothing happened. He kicked the machine and then finally yanked on the glass door. There was a snap and the door opened. Travis fell back and a golf ball-filled waterfall washed over him. He covered his head and howled.

I suppose it only took a couple of seconds, but everything was moving in slow motion. I grabbed Travis's shirt and pulled him along the floor, gliding across the water like a surfer, until I fell too. Golf balls kept flying across the room as we crawled toward the door until we could run to the car.

And, yeah, there's more about how you should always look first for security cameras and stuff like that, but I already look stupid enough.

It's a Long Story

SORRY, I thought red meant negative.

Not That I Can Think Of

WHO'S THAT you're looking for, John Silverman? No, I don't think I know any John Silverman. Now, you're not thinking of Sean Milligan, are you? No? Well, that's too bad, because Sean Milligan I used to know pretty well, though I haven't seen him in a long time, ever since that incident with the deer that got into Wilson's Furniture store. But you'd know Sean if you saw him. He's a big guy, must tip the scales at around three and a quarter, but he's got this really high-pitched voice like somebody snuck in when he was sleeping and implanted a different voice box in him.

Sean's kind of sensitive about his voice though. I remember one time, we were at that pancake breakfast the fire department has every year, and this was maybe 1999 or 2000. Must have been 1999 because it was right around the time that Prince song was playing all over the place. Do you remember that? Everyone with a TV show seemed to think they were the first one to realize how clever it would be to fade to commercial with the lyrics "party like it's 1999" playing.

Come to think of it, that Prince had a pretty high voice too. It's kind of hard to imagine Prince growing up in Minneapolis, you know what I mean. I can't help but picture him going to high school with guys like Jesse Ventura, and in my mind Prince must have spent a lot of time getting shoved into the lockers. But, you just never know, because there's Prince still selling out shows right up to the end, and then there's Jesse Ventura looking like he's one short step away from hawking jewelry on the Home Shopping Network.

It's like that time when the deer got into Wilson's Furniture store. Now, when you think of a deer you think of Bambi or maybe Rudolph, although technically I guess Rudolph is a reindeer, but basically it's the same thing: sweet disposition, big eyes, the kind of animal that looks good in animation. But those deer are wild creatures and they just don't belong in your average furniture store. Now, nobody is quite sure how that deer got into Wilson's. I mean, someone must have left a door open by the loading dock or something, and maybe the deer was lured in by the palm fronds on a coffee table display, but none of that explains how the deer made it all the way into the store without being seen. You've got to understand, you can't take more than two steps into Wilson's Furniture before the salespeople swoop down on you asking if you need any help. And that must have been what happened to Sean Milligan, because there he was feeling all full and happy after the firemen's pancake breakfast and deciding to look for a new mattress because he'd promised Molly, his wife, he'd try to get one. Molly had been complaining that their old mattress was starting to sag, which would be uncomfortable anyway, but because Sean was almost triple his wife's weight, Molly kept sliding down into the impression he left on his side of the bed, and then she had to claw herself out to the edge and she said it was like sleeping in a block of warm Jello, and she'd just had it.

So, Sean heads across the street to Wilson's, and as soon as he walks in, the salespeople swarm in on him, so he instinctively says he's "just looking," without even thinking, because when the salespeople leave he realizes that he could actually use some help. The last time he shopped for mattresses he was a kid getting dragged along by his parents. Well, Sean didn't really think this through, because as a kid the thing to do was to flop down on the mattress and see if you would bounce which would be fine if you were just a kid, but Sean, well, let's just say Sean had enough extra on him to get through a tough winter. So, when Sean flops down on the first mattress, that's a lot of pounds moving pretty quickly, and the mattress immediately breaks the legs off the bed frame, and the whole thing collapses with a huge bang that scares everyone in the store.

And that would be bad enough, but no one had noticed the deer munching on the palm fronds on the coffee table. So when the deer hears the noise, she must have thought she was being shot at because she leaps over one of those sectional sofas and starts running through the store knocking over mirrors and ottomans and those rollaway minibars you can get now. Well, everybody in the store is in a panic and this deer is hopping around like crazy looking for a way out and finally she comes over to the mattress where Sean is lying, and the deer gives him a look like she holds him personally responsible for all this, which is pretty much how Sean feels anyway, so when the deer approaches him, he lets out this scream, this sharp, high-pitched scream, kind of like that scream that Prince does at the end of "The Beautiful Ones," you know, off the *Purple Rain* album, and that really scares the deer, and she runs right through that big plate glass window in the front of the store, and that sets off the store's alarm and all the firemen who are cleaning up from the pancake breakfast come running out. Now the deer seems to be okay, but then Sean comes running out the front door and he's looking like— well, like I said, it's been a long time since I've seen Sean Milligan.

So, no, I don't think I know any John Silverman. At least, not that I can think of.

When the Aliens Arrived

WHEN THE ALIENS arrived, we didn't notice them at first, what with invisible spaceships and their chameleon-like ability to blend in with humans. But soon it became apparent that something had changed. All those creatures always staring at us, horrified by the process of eating, amazed by the yellow painted lines in the road that kept cars on either side. The aliens couldn't understand why we had to sleep, and they could never remember to stay on the sidewalk.

There were other things as well. The aliens had no interest in computers. They were afraid of elevators. The aliens stood too close when they spoke to us. They weren't polite, always asking questions about our age, our weight, and our last bowel movement.

Some of us thought that the arrival of the aliens meant the end of life as we knew it, and we hid in our homes with guns or moved to Idaho with more guns. But most of us just thought it would pass. We waited for the aliens to go back into their spaceships and fly home.

But the aliens didn't leave, and after a while we all got used to them. We began to drive more carefully, competitive spitting became a televised sport, religion became a lot more complicated, and we all began to look to the skies, watching and wondering what might happen next.

Wake

—

"GOOD MORNING," she says.

His eyelids open. He takes a deep breath.

"Hey," he says.

She sits on the edge of the bed, staring out the window.

"Tell me what you dreamed about," she says, not taking her eyes from the window.

"You know I never remember. What are you looking at out there?"

"Think."

He stretches.

"Really, I don't remember," he says.

"I always tell you about my dreams."

"I know. I hate your dreams. They always involve me chasing you with an axe or something."

She turns away from the window.

"That was one dream, and it's not like I designed it that way."

She turns back.

"But it must mean something. Otherwise you wouldn't even be interested in mine."

A ribbon of morning sunlight falls across the bed. He

moves next to her, looking out the window.

"What are you staring at out there? There's nothing but a wall and some wires."

"Okay, then, you tell me. What does it mean when I dream that you chase me with an axe?"

"I don't know. Maybe you're scared of me. Or maybe I represent something you're afraid you can't control."

"Don't flatter yourself."

"You tell me then. Why would I chase you with an axe?"

"Maybe you're afraid of me. Maybe you're projecting your fear, coming after me before I can come after you. How's that sound?"

Quiet. And then they speak at the same time.

"I Let's WANT go TO back BREAK to UP bed."

Iron Chef Dishwasher

THIS IS ALTON BROWN in Kitchen Stadium where the conclusion of Battle Blueberry saw Iron Chef Bobby Flay defeat challenger Philippe Excoffier in a contest that featured blueberry tarts, blueberry-seared steaks, and a kiwi/blueberry sorbet that proved the judges' favorite. And that can mean only one thing . . .

It's time for *Iron Chef Dishwasher*, a contest in which two of the nation's finest *plongeurs* clean up the veritable mountain of pans, dishes, and cooking implements left behind by tonight's *Iron Chef* competition. Judging by the caked-on, spattered, and burnt-beyond-recognition blueberries that make Kitchen Stadium look like a crime scene after a delicious shooting, we are in for quite a battle.

Tonight, mopping up for Iron Chef Flay is Iron Chef Dishwasher Mikey Lynch, who has polished the plates at Manhattan's Gourmand, Brooklyn's Fresh Catch, and the Riker's Island commissary. Chef Excoffier's mess will be cleaned up by challenger Angela Jackson, who has lent her scouring talents to some of the finest diners along the old Route 66, including Sid's, Hammie's, and the Truck Full Stop.

And there's the bell announcing that the cleanup has begun. Let's go down to the floor to my colleague and wing man, Kevin Brauch. Kevin, what do you see?

Thanks, Alton. Well, our contestants aren't wasting any time. Iron Chef Dishwasher Lynch is right in the belly of the beast. He's taken cookie sheets that Iron Chef Flay inexplicably used to broil steaks on, and he's soaking them in water hot enough to cook lobsters. But will that be enough to ever get them clean again? Back to you, Alton.

Thank you, Kevin. Meanwhile on Dishwasher Jackson's side, she has taken pans that Chef Excoffier used to poach a blueberry chipotle salmon and placed them into the sink. But she's not putting any water into them. No, she's actually pouring vinegar and baking soda right onto the surface. That's right, watch the lava flow, kids. It's a high school science fair. Now she's adding a little water to the mix, hoping that better living through chemistry will clear out the blueberry gunk.

Meanwhile, Mikey Lynch is going after the cake pan from the lemon blueberry buckle, a strudel-type pastry that the judges earlier thought was slightly overcooked. From the look on Dishwasher Lynch's face, I believe he would agree. He's going after the bottom of that pan with a stainless steel scouring pad. He's going to get quite an upper body workout on that buckle.

The challenger now seems to be soaking the rest of her pans, and she has moved on to the dishes and cutlery. The dishwashing machines are open and packed with detergent and she's starting to load them up, but I see a problem here. The ridiculously shaped oblong soup bowls that Chef Excoffier used for the blueberry-squash-lobster bisque will not fit on the top rack of the dishwasher. Angela Jackson is going to need to load them into the lower rack and that will cost her time.

As we near the midway point of tonight's competition, I'm being told that we've got a surprise. Let's turn it over to Kevin.

Yes, Alton. Check out what Dishwasher Lynch is doing to treat the china glasses that were earlier glazed with a mixed berry compote. You'll remember that the compote went with a brioche French toast, but as a timesaver the compote had been baked directly in the china. That has left blueberries scorched onto the glasses, and the champion is treating the surface of with a mixture of vinegar, lemon juice, black tea, and—yes, it is—Coca-Cola. Alton.

Thank you, Kevin. We always say here in Kitchen Stadium, once you see what a glass of Coke does to a rusty nail, you'll never drink it again. Over on the challenger's side, Angela Jackson is working on wine glasses that held tonight's blueberry peach sangria. Remember that dishwashers are scored not only on cleanliness and lack of breakage but also by whether or not water spots remain on glasses. The challenger is hand inspecting each glass before loading it into the dishwasher. And look, she's just caught sight of a lipstick stain on one of the glasses. That must be judge Karine Bakhoum's glass, and if I'm correct that lipstick shade is

Dior Creme de Rose Balm. Dishwasher Jackson is placing the glass over a boiling kettle of water, holding the glass by the stem as it fogs up. Now she is wiping the glass with a paper towel. And, yes, the lipstick is gone, but I need to make a correction. I have been told that the lipstick shade was in fact the Tarte LipSurgence Matte Lip Tint.

As we near the end of this battle, our champion has his machines loaded and running, but he still has to deal with the pans that have been soaking, including the griddle that was used for the sweet corn and potato latkes with blueberry lavender sauce. The judges thought the latkes were delicious, but the griddle looks like the set of a slasher movie. Wait a second! Is he using a metal scouring pad on a non-stick griddle. Oooh, that is a big no-no and it is going to cost him.

In the last few minutes, the challenger is cleaning the stovetop, and we can see the different training each *plongeur* has had at play. Dishwasher Jackson is working with Goo Gone Multi-Purpose Cleaner and just covering that stove top with it. Whew! I can feel the fumes from here, and they are making my eyes water. But Dishwasher Lynch is sticking with the tried-and-true Arm & Hammer baking soda, which he is shaking onto the stovetop and scrubbing with a wet cloth. It takes a little more elbow grease, but look at that stove shine.

We are in our final few moments. The dishwashers are quickly sweeping floors and clearing counters. Any second now, it won't look like any food was even prepared here.

5 – 4 – 3 – 2 – 1. Hands up! It's finished. We'll be back with the results after—oh, wait, wrong show. We'll all just go home now.

I'm on Fire

PLACING HIS vodka gimlet on the bar, Simon exhaled smoke and straightened the sleeve of his new Italian shirt. He knew he looked good tonight, and he was ready to make the most of "ladies night" at the Loose Goose.

As Simon surveyed the room, he spied clusters of women huddled around tables of Polynesian drinks. His attention focused on a leggy blonde sitting alone across the bar, working on her second margarita. Their eyes met. Maybe she'd be the one.

Simon lurched forward as a plump brunette bumped into him on her way to the bar. *Christ*, he thought, *why don't you wait at the trough for the feed bucket?* He tried to take a drag from his cigarette but saw that it had gone out. He decided to re-light his cigarette using a matchbook trick he'd seen in a movie. But first he had to make sure that blonde was still checking him out. Of course, she was. *And she should be*, Simon thought, *because tonight, I'm on fire.*

Suddenly the blonde pointed at him and screamed, "You're on fire!"

Simon spun around to look in the mirror he knew was

on the wall behind him. A ball of flame perched on top of his head, a burst of fire that was redder than the hair of whatshername he'd hooked up with last week. Instinctively, Simon plunged to floor, beating his hair with his hands and banging his head against the tile. In the seconds before he knocked himself out, Simon thought he smelled omelets, but only later did he realize that the cigarette ash had ignited the egg white base in his homemade hair mousse. He went through a dozen eggs a week for his hair, but he realized as he was slipping into unconsciousness that he hadn't had an omelet since his mother had last cooked him breakfast.

In the days that followed, as Simon lay in bed recovering from second-degree burns to his hands and head and a mild concussion, his thoughts returned to that leggy blonde.

He would never know that what she remembered about Simon was not his clothes, not his hair (even after it went up in flames), not even the way that, after regaining consciousness, Simon insisted that the paramedics carry him to the ambulance on a stretcher. No, what she remembered was the sound of Simon's scream when he realized he was on fire. It was a high-pitched, insistent squeal that didn't quite sound human. It reminded her of Bernie, the hamster from her childhood. Bernie had loved the running wheel in his cage. He would scamper on it for hours, his little paws extended in full gallop, his mouth open wide making the same sound she'd heard that guy on fire make.

She had really loved that hamster. That night, she softly cried herself to sleep, wishing she could still hear the whirl of the wheel and Bernie's shriek as he rode it once again.

The Zone

THE ZONE is a semi-circular arc that exists around our daughter, Emily. It emanates out from Emily like an invisible aura defined by the distance of her reach. Emily, though only two, understands The Zone. At least she realizes that all items falling inside The Zone are eligible for play or ingestion. This is why our son Jordan's favorite toy, now called "Choking Hazard Man," must always remain in his room.

So, one morning, when my wife and I take Emily out with us for breakfast after dropping Jordan off at school, our initial actions all demonstrate respect for The Zone. After walking into Mykonos Diner and picking out a table as far away from the smoking section as possible, I buckle Emily into the high chair while my wife takes out a wipe from the diaper bag and sanitizes the high chair and table. Then, while she takes out a plastic bowl with Cheerios, I remove all objects of interest from The Zone: sugar packets, napkins, pads of butter, water glasses, and the tip from the previous customer. My failure, say, by leaving a saltshaker inside The Zone, will lead to Emily unscrewing the shaker and leaving an anthill-sized salt mound on the table.

A waitress approaches. Jennifer, according to her nametag. Jennifer smiles at us warmly, but she places a set of silverware right in the middle of The Zone. Emily immediately takes up a knife, waving it in the air with Ninja-like skills and evading our attempts to disarm her. Jennifer asks if we want anything to drink. While my wife distracts Emily with a stuffed animal, I reach over and pluck the knife from Emily's hand, placing it outside The Zone. Jennifer stands, hand on hip, impatiently waiting. We order coffee and attempt to restore order.

Servers, particularly those with children of their own, often have an implicit understanding of The Zone, and they will assist us in piling up one end of the table with side orders of toast, jugs of syrup, and extra cups of juice. However, it soon becomes clear that Jennifer sees The Zone simply as available space. When she returns, she places a coffee pot right in front of Emily. The coffee pot is a bright Day-Glo orange, the universal sign for decaf, but in the eyes of our daughter it is a shiny bauble come rightfully into her possession.

We lurch forward. Six hands struggle for control of the coffee pot.

Jennifer smiles, waiting for our order.

"Cute kid."

Bet You

———

GOING TO DAYTONA BEACH for spring break had to be the stupidest thing Lucas did his sophomore year, well, at least his first sophomore year. Almost two years later, his MasterCard was still maxed out, and making this month's minimum payment left him with almost nothing to live on until the next paycheck from his work-study job. Sometimes it felt like he would never be out of debt.

He did the math and figured that if he lived on pasta he could make it through the week, but then he remembered that he had plans to go out with John and Brandon tonight. Lucas opened up his wallet and sighed. $4.88 wouldn't go far, but if he bought a glass of cheap beer and nursed it, he'd get through the night.

Lucas threw on his jacket and slipped through the icy streets down to the College View Cafe. The bar windows were steamed up. When he opened the door, heat and noise poured out. He scanned the crowded room and saw his friends sitting at the table in the back.

"Lucas! Luke! Lukey! Sacul backwards! Waaa-haa!"

It looked like they had started without him, and then he saw why. Miller was there. Lucas didn't really like Miller, but because they hung out with a lot of the same people they had become friends by default. Miller had graduated on time and gotten this big deal chemist job in the industrial park, so he usually didn't come slumming down by the college.

"Lucas, long time no see, buddy. S'up?" Miller threw his arm around Lucas's shoulder.

"No complaints, Miller. Yourself?"

"Living for the weekend but starting on it early. Hey, you need a glass. This round's on me."

"Round?" Lucas asked.

"Yeah, I can't believe you losers drink that weasel piss." He held up his glass. It glowed amber under the fluorescent lights of the bar. "Here's a beer you might actually want to drink."

Lucas took off his hat and coat and sat down while Miller flagged down a waitress.

"Can we get another glass for our friend here? And, he's behind. Bring him an Amoco?"

Lucas looked up. "What's an Amoco?"

"Don't worry. It's on me, pal."

Everyone seemed pretty far gone. John and Brandon were red faced and quiet. Miller told a story about some people Lucas didn't know. The waitress returned and placed a shot glass in front of him. The liquid in it was clear except for a brown drop floating on the surface.

"What is this?"

"C'mon, grandma. Just shoot it."

Lucas picked up the shot and tried to swallow it as quickly as he could. His throat burned and his stomach convulsed. Tears came to his eyes and he started coughing. Everyone at the table laughed. Miller slapped him on the back.

"Hey, you want me to ask the waitress for a glass of milk?"

"Funny," Lucas wheezed. "What was in that?"

"I think it's 151 and Kahlua. Maybe something else." Miller poured the rest of the pitcher into his glass. "John, you on for the next pitcher? This soldier is honorably discharged."

"Uh, yeah, I guess so," John said, pulling a ten out of his pocket. Lucas then realized that the next round would be coming his way and he wouldn't be able to pay for it. Maybe if he was with just John and Brandon, he could beg off. But if Miller saw that he couldn't afford to buy a pitcher of beer, he'd hear about it for the rest of his life. He needed an out. Lucas started thinking fast. But it was hard to think with Miller going on about the good old days.

"Yeah, remember that party at Chi Rho, that one with the kiddie pool filled with grain punch. Brandon here does a belly flop into the pool. Smooth, Brandon."

Brandon got all flustered, like he usually did. "I was pushed. I didn't dive in."

Miller ignored him. "You're lucky you didn't get alcohol poisoning or go blind or something. There was this—"

Lucas interrupted Miller. "I bet you I can drink a shot of

straight grain alcohol."

"What? You're whacked."

"I'll bet you the next pitcher I can do it." Lucas stared right at Miller.

Miller stared back. "You're on."

Miller had the waitress bring over a shot of Everclear and a water chaser. She set them in front of Lucas. By sight, there wasn't any difference between the grain alcohol and the glass of water. Slowly, he lowered his hand and picked up the shot. He took a breath.

Lucas put the shot glass to his lips and threw his head back. At first he just felt the sensation of liquid in his mouth and throat. But then his throat constricted and he couldn't breathe. Lucas lurched for the glass of water, but he knocked it over. Water washed over the tabletop. He threw himself to his knees, put his lips to the table, and began sucking up water. He used his hands to wipe more liquid from the table into his mouth. Suddenly the bar was very quiet. Lucas stopped swallowing and looked up. Everyone in the bar was staring at him.

Miller spoke. "You know, we studied this in Intro to Chemistry freshman year. Ethanol gets absorbed through the mucous membranes in the mouth. But each ethanol molecule will chemically lock onto six molecules of water. So, the water in your mouth and throat gets sucked up by the grain alcohol instantly. It has this massive dehydrating effect. It can even destroy your brain at high doses."

Lucas looked at Miller. Water dripped from Lucas' chin

onto his shirt. He felt like he had swallowed a hand gre-
nade.

"Anyway," Miller said, signaling for a waitress. "That
was worth a round."

Pop Song Carbon Footprints

"Light My Fire"
by the Doors

The time to hesitate is through.
No time to wallow in the mire.
Try now we can only lose,
And our love become a funeral pyre,
Come on, baby, light my fire.

Carbon footprint: A traditional open-air funeral pyre burns for around six hours, using approximately 385 lbs. of wood. A single funeral pyre produces 362.25 lbs. of CO_2, and in India four million tons of wood are used annually for traditional cremations.

"Rock'n Me"
by Steve Miller Band

I went from Phoenix, Arizona
All the way to Tacoma
Philadelphia, Atlanta, L.A.,

Northern California where the girls are warm
So I could hear my sweet baby say
Keep on a rock'n me baby.

Carbon footprint: 2,358 lbs. of CO_2 emissions (all flights economy class). The overall footprint would be less if a car was used, but Steve Miller Band also released the song "Jet Airliner."

"Midnight Train to Georgia"
by Gladys Knight & the Pips

L.A. proved too much for the man,
So he's leavin' the life he's come to know,
He said he's goin' back to find
Ooh, what's left of his world,
The world he left behind
Not so long ago.
He's leaving
On that midnight train to Georgia.

Carbon footprint: Only 132 lbs. of CO_2 emissions (Amtrak from Los Angeles to Atlanta via New Orleans). Note: there currently is no midnight train to Georgia from Los Angeles. The above calculation is for the 3 P.M. Sunset Limited. There is a 6:15 P.M. departure from Los Angeles, but that train is less direct, connecting through Chicago and Washington, D. C.

"I Can't Drive 55"
by Sammy Hagar

One foot on the brake and one on the gas, hey!
Well, there's too much traffic, I can't pass, no!
So I tried my best illegal move
A big black and white come and crushed my groove again!

Go on & write me up for 125
Post my face, wanted dead or alive
Take my license n' all that jive
I can't drive 55! Oh no! Uh!

Carbon footprint: A 1983 Ferrari 512 Boxer (the car used in the "I Can't Drive 55" video) that gets an average of 14.7 miles per gallon highway and is driven a typical 12,000 miles per year uses 816 gallons of gasoline and produces 15,836 lbs. of CO_2 emissions. If driven at 125 miles per hour, the Ferrari 512 Boxer would get an estimated average mpg of no more than 5.0 miles per gallon. Over a year, Sammy Hagar would use 2,400 gallons of gas and produce 46,560 lbs. of CO_2.

Nice Off

As STEPHEN held the leash and waited for his dog to do his business, a Nice Off began on the corner of 18th and College streets. Stephen had lived in this town long enough that he knew better than to get involved, so he just stood back and watched it transpire. At the four-way stop, two cars pulled up. The red car on College Street arrived first. It was a Buick driven by a grandfatherly looking man. A split second later, a silver minivan reached the white line at the stop sign on 18th Street. It was piloted by what looked to be a young mother wearing exceptionally large sunglasses.

And then the Nice Off began. Both cars hovered, waiting for the other to pass through the intersection, not wanting to seem rude. Of course, the red car had the right of way, having arrived first, but clearly the Buick grandfather felt the gentlemanly thing to do was to let the minivan Mom go first. Minivan Mom, of course, was not going to jump out ahead of an elderly man.

Neither vehicle budged, suspended by the force of their politeness.

On to round two. The drivers gazed at one another and smiled, hoping that that acknowledgement would be enough for the other to admit defeat and pull through the intersection. However, each driver remained convinced of his or her superior niceness, and the Round of Smiles ended in a draw. Other cars approached the crossroads, lining up behind the combatants.

The Nice Off then moved into the Round of Waving. The Buick grandfather flicked his wrist toward the minivan Mom and grinned, as if to gently nudge her forward, like he would have led a dance partner onto the floor back in the day. Simultaneously, the minivan Mom turned her palm upward, raising the ante by mouthing the words "you, go" through her smile with the same gentle encouragement she likely used when toilet training her children. But the Buick grandfather deflected her parry and responded with a carefully annunciated "no, no, you." His grin seemed to spread even more widely across his face, if such a thing was possible.

Clearly an impasse had been reached, and it was more than Stephen could bear to watch. The drivers were in agony, and the inability of either's niceness to prevail was palpable in the pain it caused. Stephen couldn't bear to witness such suffering any longer. He gave a yank on his dog's leash and walked into the intersection, right in front of the silver minivan. Both drivers froze and stared. The Buick grandfather had no choice now. He edged off the brake and began crawling forward through the intersection. Stephen cast a friendly wave toward the Buick as it passed, then turned his head and mimed "thank you" to the befuddled face of the minivan Mom. Stephen crossed the street with what could only be described as a strut because he knew that he had won the Nice Off.

The Time of My Life

REMEMBER TO SUCK in your stomach. That's the most important thing, particularly because you're wearing a bikini. Smile, too, of course. You don't want to look like you're at a funeral when you're at the beach. Try not to squint, even though you're staring into the sun and it makes you feel even more nauseous than you already feel. Maybe you shouldn't have done those shots of tequila last night. Or maybe something was wrong with the Chinese food. Or maybe it was the worm in the tequila.

You're not ready when the picture is taken, so you tell Sami to take another, because your phone's camera isn't working, but Sami has already moved up the beach, and so now the only sign of your spring break trip (besides the Visa bill) is this stupid picture where you look hung over and flabby and unhappy, and the main problem is that the picture is accurate. That's exactly how you feel, because Florida really wasn't much fun after all, and you spent so much money that now you're thinking about donating plasma so you can make your next car payment.

Then when your dad walks into your room and looks at the picture on your computer screen, he says, "I told you it wouldn't be worth it." You don't say anything at first, because that's exactly what you thought, and you can't give him the satisfaction of being right. But saying nothing is like agreeing with him because then he goes on to tell you—again—about how he worked his way through college and sent money home to help out his younger brothers and sisters. Like it's your fault for being an only child.

"Oh, it was worth it, all right," you say, which sounds lame, even to you. "It was the time of my life. You just don't want me to have fun because you need a judge's permission to leave the state."

As soon as the words leave your mouth, you wish you could hit a delete key, because you've broken the unspoken family rule not to mention your dad being on probation. And it's kind of a cheap shot anyway, since you know that the money your dad took from investors went into trying to keep his business afloat during the recession. He didn't benefit from it, even if it was technically embezzlement.

But your dad just gives you this sick look, a look not all that different from the one on your face in that picture on that beach, and he walks out of the room, and you don't get a chance to apologize because that's the night your dad moves out for good. You feel bad, but when you visit your dad at his new apartment on the other side of town, it never seems like the right time to say you are sorry. On one level, on a rational level, you realize that he didn't move out because of what you said. He and your mom had been planning to separate for a while. In fact, maybe that was what he had been coming into your room to tell you, but you can't help but feel responsible for his leaving, and now when you look at that picture from the beach, all you see is shame.

Terminal

—————

IT WAS HIS own fault, of course, for not paying close attention when he booked the return leg of his flight. He should have double-checked the boarding pass when he printed it off. But, still, someone in the chain-of-command should have spotted the problem. After all, he was just an amateur traveler, a passenger and nothing more. The professionals in customer service and transportation screening—the many people who asked to see his ID once he got to the airport—wouldn't you have thought one of them would have noticed that he had shown up at 6:00 A.M. for a flight that didn't leave until 7:45 P.M.?

After all, he couldn't have been the first person who clicked P.M. instead of A.M. when booking a flight online? It hadn't been a difficult mistake to make, but apparently it was not one that was easily noticed. Being sleep deprived and a little hungover when he had gotten to the airport, all he had wanted was a cup of coffee and a few rounds of Angry Birds on his phone. But the coffee was too hot, and he couldn't unlock this one level no matter what he catapulted at those damn pigs. By the time he stopped to look up, it was 7:30 A.M. and he ran around in a panic, worried that he would miss his flight.

But he couldn't find his flight on the departure screens. That was when he stopped and read his boarding pass more carefully, and then he read it again. It took a third read before his situation became clear. He hadn't missed his flight. It just didn't leave for another twelve hours.

He went back to the ticket counter and pleaded his case. They offered him standby on an earlier flight, but they weren't hopeful about his getting on. It was possible to reconnect, but who wanted to fly from Minneapolis to Chicago with connections in Denver and Dallas? He decided to accept his fate.

Maybe they would have let him out past security, but what would he have done with an extra 12 hours in the city anyway? He didn't have a hotel room and it was barely 20 degrees outside. There was no place for him to go.

So, he tried to make the most of it. He had some eggs and toast, watched a few planes take off, and got halfway through the *USA Today* crossword puzzle. He walked the length of the terminal, watched people go through screening, and ate a second breakfast. It was only 10 A.M.

He found a quiet alcove and tried to take a nap, but he had had too much coffee and he was feeling kind of jittery. He thought maybe he would do some push-ups. But the alcove turned out to be a staff entrance, and he almost got run over by a maintenance cart.

Had he known he would be spending the day in the airport, he would have done a few things differently, like pack his phone charger. After another round of Angry Birds, he realized his battery was running low. He got his shoes shined, bought a neck pillow, and found out that he didn't like Rev7, the new biodegradable gum.

At midday, the terminal got more crowded. He tried to put off having lunch so that he'd have something to look forward to, but he got hungry earlier than he would have thought. Or maybe it was just the smell of chalupas. Either way, he had to fight for a table in the food court when he sat down to eat.

He found himself staring at people, looking for a familiar face in hopes that he would see someone he knew. It was lonely eating lunch by himself. But that feeling didn't last. Around 1:30 he started to hate humanity. People were rude, some of them smelled, all of them had too much carry-on baggage. He just wanted to be alone, but that was an absolute impossibility. He had to settle for slouching across a near-empty row of seats, blocking the aisle with his legs.

It was hard to determine exactly when things got interesting. It could have been when he saw the eight-foot man holding hands with the four-foot woman, though that wasn't beyond the realm of possibility. By the time little miniature coffee pots started to float past him in soap bubbles, he realized something was happening.

He should have been scared, or at least concerned, to see purple giraffes working the counter at Starbucks, but it was actually a relief. At least that was interesting. By 6 P.M.

he thought he should make his way over to his departure gate, and he wondered how many somersaults it would take to get there: 72, as it turned out. He found this fascinating if a little dizzying, but the security guard he spoke to wasn't as impressed.

It was time to make friends. He introduced himself to his fellow passengers at the gate by asking for everyone's Social Security number. This time he got to meet a different security guard. This guard's name was Cheryl, and she was nice enough to stay with him until his plane was ready to board. As he stood in line clutching his boarding pass, he realized that he hadn't seen anything at all. He had spent the whole day in the terminal, but what did he really know about this airport? Who had built it? How did it function? How could he leave without knowing anything? He hesitated, holding up the line and gripping his boarding pass tightly. Cheryl asked if he wanted to go for a walk. They walked.

What Kind of Person

NATHAN HAD to stop and ask himself just what kind of person he was. Was he the sort of person who was running late and needed to cash a check quickly so that he wouldn't miss his ride down to the concert in Iowa City, and who therefore would cut in front of the old and extremely slow woman ahead of him on the sidewalk between the parking lot and the entrance to the bank?

Or was he the type who, even though he was running late and just needed to cash a check quickly, would make a point of holding the door to the bank for the old and now even more extremely slow woman, letting her go in ahead of him?

It really wasn't much of a question.

So, he forced a smile onto his face as he held the door open for the old woman and nodded as he accepted her thanks while she made her way into the bank—though it would be more accurate to say that if glaciers melted as slowly as the old woman moved, then global warming would not be much of a concern after all.

Finally, when both Nathan and the woman entered the lobby of the bank, Nathan debated whether he could then cut ahead of her to the only teller whose station was open. But, no, what would be the point of having proven himself to be the kind of person who holds doors open for old women, if he then blew by her the way he would rush the stage at the concert in Iowa City, if he didn't miss his ride, which it increasingly looked like he would, as he stood behind the old woman and watched her painstakingly unfold a piece of paper and struggle to read her own handwriting?

Nathan stood, trying not to squirm or tap his foot too loudly, while the woman asked the teller, "Has 8511 cleared? Yes? . . . But 8513 has not cleared? Okay, then what's the balance in savings?"

The teller offered to write it down.

"No, no, you can just tell me." The woman appeared to prefer conversation, since that was the slowest possible manner by which to get things done. Nathan checked his phone to assure himself that it only seemed as if time had come to a stop.

The teller's voice dropped but not so low that Nathan couldn't hear.

"You have 97,356 dollars and 18 cents in savings."

Wait, what? Nathan almost asked out loud. He couldn't help but lean closer.

"Oh, is it that much?" the woman replied. "Then let's transfer . . . make it $75,000 into checking, and I'd like to withdraw 42 dollars in cash."

Wait, how much? Nathan was confused and found himself appraising the woman's clothing more carefully for some sign that she was as rich as she apparently was. But he recognized her clothes as those he often had stocked on shelves while working the overnight shift at Target. How had this woman not realized she had accumulated almost $100,000 in a savings account? What kind of person casually transferred $75,000 and withdrew $42 in the same sentence?

Nathan kept his head down and tried to look like he wasn't paying attention. The effort worked because he found himself fantasizing that the old woman would turn away from the teller and present him with a check for tens of thousands of dollars in recognition of his politeness. No, she would turn away from the teller and ask if she could adopt him so that he could inherit her millions and reside as a Lord on a British country estate.

Then the woman actually did turn away from the teller, and she smiled at him. Nathan grinned back, happy, so happy to once again see the face of his benefactor, a woman whom he had, over the course of their acquaintance, come to not only admire but respect.

"You're next," she said, and she slowly shuffled by him. Suddenly, he realized that that was it. She was going to walk away. He watched her leave in disbelief, and it was all he could do to turn back to the teller and give her the check in his hand.

"Do you want two $10s or a $20?" the teller asked.

"Uh . . . two $10s," Nathan replied.

"Okay—oops, I'll need to get some more tens from the

vault. It'll just take a couple minutes. You're not in a rush, are you?

"Oh, no. No rush."

Testimony

I WISH FIRST to address the scurrilous rumors of which I am sure you are all aware. Rather than dignify these rumors by repeating them, let me simply emphasize that at no time did male executives of our company engage in sexual conduct involving female prostitutes and winged animals of both sexes. Despite press reports to the contrary, there was no videotape of such sexual encounters taking place at our corporate headquarters, nor did I order the destruction of any such videotape.

You may also be aware of photographs circulating on the Internet that purport to show executives of our company engaged in the forms of sexual conduct just noted. I assure you that these pictures obviously have been doctored, particularly in the addition of the endangered American bald eagle to photographs of alleged sexual activity. Though, in fact, the American bald eagle does appear on our corporate logo and letterhead, no one from our company has had any physical contact whatsoever with an actual American bald eagle. It is our corporate policy that no animals are to be harmed by any of our business practices, even those that are not, technically, business related.

Let me repeat that despite all the wild rumors, the doctored photographs—and, yes, notwithstanding the bird feathers recovered by police—there has been no conclusive evidence offered that shows that any of the activities described above did in fact occur.

Now, I know my purpose in being here today is not to discuss these rumors, but I felt it necessary to address, in a forthright and open manner, accusations that I have felt—to use a phrase that may not be entirely appropriate in this context—were hanging like an albatross around my neck.

For the record, I want you all to know how saddened my family and I have been by the pain caused by our company's recent setbacks. Despite what you may have read, I have not been aloof and isolated in the face of mass layoffs and the collapse of our employee retirement portfolio. As the founder of this company, I personally have suffered through every firing and each drop in our stock price. Though I should note that I no longer hold significant shares of stock in the company and, in addition, the nature of my position kept me out of day-to-day decision-making for the company during the period under current criminal investigation. So while I have been deeply affected by these events, I have had no personal responsibility for them.

At this point, Senators, I would like to extend myself to answer questions you may have. I must note that, on the advice of counsel, I will afford myself of the protections provided for me by our Constitution in regard to questions relating to the company, my sale of company shares, or any other item currently or potentially under criminal investigation. In all other matters, I am an open book.

Pete

"I'VE GOT TO GET another job," Pete muttered to himself as he sloshed the mop across the classroom floor. It was still hard to believe that he was back in St. Gotteschalk Elementary. Fifteen years ago, he had been a student here, and now he wanted to strangle the kids who left wads of gum under their desks, kids like the one he had been.

He felt bad now about having stuck crayons into the grooves of Teresa Griffin's shoes so that she left a trail of red-orange and sky blue as she walked down the hall. He felt even worse about the time he had put a pack of ketchup under Vinnie Cardini's chair. Somebody had to clean that shit up, you know, and now he was that somebody.

Suddenly Pete spun around, threw his mop to the ground, and pointed toward the empty chair at the desk that had been his in fifth grade. "Quit screwing around," Pete shouted. "Pay enough attention so you can get a decent job. And don't think you can just become a welder like your dad because somebody's going to invent computers that'll weld just about everything."

Pete stormed over to his old desk and pounded his fist on it. "And, whatever the hell you do, stay away from *her*."

He pointed two rows over to the desk where Michelle Lorraine had sat. "Yeah, I know what you're thinking about her, and you know what? In about five years, she's going to look even better. But you'll spend most of high school chasing after her, and, when you finally start going out with her, she'll sleep with your best friend."

Pete sighed and pushed his old desk up against the wall before picking the mop back up. He dropped the mop into the bucket, wrung out the excess, and started swabbing the floor again. It was just too weird working here at St. Gotteschalk and, being alone at night, he couldn't stop his mind from wandering where he didn't want it to go.

He had thought this would just be a temporary gig when he took it, but that was almost a year ago. Here he was, still keeping the school and church clean, fixing broken chair legs in the rectory, and making special trips to the supply closet for light bulbs for the nuns (he couldn't believe how often the nuns bothered him for more light bulbs). But the worst part—the thing Pete couldn't get over—was the fact that they didn't trust him. When there was a break-in last month and the school's new computers were stolen, he was the main suspect. It was a good thing he'd gone to the hockey game with his brother the night of the break-in, because without an alibi they might have fired him. You'd think that after being in this parish his whole life, he would have earned some kind of respect, but the nuns still looked at him like he was a kid who'd shoot a spitball as soon as their backs were turned.

Pete heard the sound of a door slamming. It was probably just Father Michael coming by to check up on him. Another one who didn't trust him, didn't respect him. He kept mopping so that Father Michael would walk in and see him hard at work, but no one came by. That was funny. Pete was sure he had heard a door slam. He went over and stuck his head into the hallway. All the lights were off, but there was a flicker of light at the end of the hallway. He listened closely and thought he heard whispers.

It's another break-in, Pete thought. His cell phone was in his jacket on the other side of the building. The only other phones were in the main office, down where the voices were coming from, so there was no way he could call the cops. Of course, he could have just gone out the back entrance, run over to the rectory, and woken up Father Michael. That would have been the easy thing to do. That would have been the smart thing to do.

But Pete looked at the mop in his hand, and he knew what had to be done. He twisted the handle out of the mop end, turned off the lights in the room, and quietly made his way down the hall, holding the mop handle like a samurai sword. The door to the main office was open. People inside were whispering. It sounded like there were at least four of them, huddled behind the door of a supply cabinet. They had him outnumbered, but he had surprise on his side. Pete tiptoed into the office, took a deep breath, and raised the mop handle. He flipped on the light switch and jumped toward the cabinet, screaming "Aaaaaaaa!!" only to see

Sister Margaret and Sister Judy, his third- and first-grade teachers, respectively, holding light bulbs in their hands.

What happened next felt like a dream to Pete. He remembered dropping the mop handle. There was the sound of light bulbs shattering on the floor, and, of course, the screams of Sister Margaret and Sister Judy (he would never forget the screams). He kept thinking that there had to be burglars still somewhere in the office; he knew that there had to be, and he kept searching for them in corners and under desks. But it was so hard to move. It was like there were weights attached to him. Or was someone grabbing him? He thought maybe Father Michael had asked him something, but then Father Michael was a doctor asking for his name. And there were flashes of light from the burglars' flashlight or was it from something the doctor was holding? He wasn't sure the burglars had a flashlight now. No, there was only one thing that he knew for certain. He was sure that he was going to Hell.

Each and Every Pose

GOOD MORNING, everyone. I'm Sandy and I'll be filling in for Monica for today's Beginning Yoga class. I hope some of you remember me from the last time I subbed back before I got married. That's right, I'm now a newlywed. Oh, thank you. Yes, it's been wonderful.

Well, let's start with a sun salutation. Inhale up. Exhale back. Float down. Draw your head toward your knees—you can bend your knees a little if you have limited flexibility in your hamstring, and . . . hold.

Now, if you want to see limited flexibility, let's talk about my sister-in-law. She practically ruined the whole wedding.

Okay, inhale up, exhale down, and step back into a plank position. Your palms should be nicely grounded. Hold that.

Can you believe my sister-in-law told us she wouldn't even come to the wedding unless we paid to fly her out? I mean, have you ever heard of such a thing?

Drop your knees down and unfold your toes. Stretch and lengthen your spine by drawing your hips back into a child position. Keep breathing deeply.

I can appreciate that my sister-in-law hasn't been doing

well since her divorce. But it was just a mistake for her to start a pet sitting service without knowing that she was allergic to cats.

And let's move into a cat stretch. On your hands and knees in neutral position. This is a great stretch for both your spine and paraspinal muscles. Slowly move your back down, arch your back, and bring your head up. Hold for a count of three. One . . . two . . . —

It would be one thing if we had had a destination wedding like we had initially hoped, but we were getting married in my husband's hometown, and still, every penny we had was going into this wedding. We tried to make it easier by telling her that just her presence would be gift enough. But that didn't help things at all.

And relax.

Now, let's work on our core strength. Back into neutral position. Let's take the right arm and left leg and extend them. Square your hips, keep the arm near the ear, level with your shoulder. Remember to breathe. And hold.

I can't tell you how many hours I spent online trying to find her the cheapest airline ticket. And I was literally in tears every time I got off the phone with her.

Back to neutral position and let's reverse sides. Extend the left arm and right leg, focusing on maintaining your balance.

I mean, it got to a point where I was practically ready to elope. And my husband would not talk to his sister. They've never gotten along particularly well, and he's just not someone who does conflict.

Great. Relax. Now draw your shoulders down. Add in some gentle shoulder roles. Be mindful of how they feel. We all carry a lot of tension in the shoulder area. A lot of anxiety gets stuck there.

Finally, after I don't know how many hours of phone calls and discussions, we decided—and this was my husband's suggestion initially—we decided to make things easier on everyone and just uninvite my sister-in-law.

So, let's go into a warrior pose. Rotate your hips until they are squared front, then lunge forward with your right foot. Slowly extend your arms straight up. Feel every limb of your body expand and elongate. Feel the removal of all your obstacles. And hold.

Well, from the way everyone reacted you would have thought we had tried to kidnap my sister-in-law's child or something. More phone calls, more tears. And that was just from my mother-in-law, who had now gotten involved.

Keep holding.

But I was not going to budge at this point. I had had it up to here with my sister-in-law, and frankly with my husband's whole family.

Okay, relax.

Let's all sit down, gaze upward to your fingertips, and reach for the sky. Inhale up and exhale down. Let your body and mind be invigorated. Up and down. Keep going.

Finally, my mother-in-law said she would pay for her daughter's plane ticket if we re-invited her. And I have to tell you, I wasn't sure about it at first, after all of the trouble and stress she had caused us. But finally my husband gave in—he just can't stand up to his mother—and I guess I was persuaded that it would be for the best to have everyone in the family at the wedding, or we'd have to explain why my sister-in-law wasn't in the pictures every time we brought out the wedding album. So, in the end, she was there, and I think she had wonderful time at the reception, at least judging by all she had to drink.

Okay, let's shake out your legs and bring them center. Breathe deeply, several breaths.

So, did anyone watch *The Bachelor* last night? Did you? Can you believe the nerve of the guy this season? He's not even all that cute. I don't know what he's thinking.

All right, final stretch. Please move into a relaxed position. Remember, yoga poses should not feel stressful. The idea is to relax in each and every pose and go to your edge. Then, after a few breaths, you go beyond that edge.

Hit Single

DAVID LEANED UP against his amp in a fetal position. A full morning of telemarketing didn't quite cover his share of the rehearsal space tonight. Every minute not rehearsing was another telephone call about the benefits of aluminum siding.

When the band had been a handful of guys just stringing together gigs, it didn't really matter. But now that two different labels had contacted them, things had changed. And everything was riding on next week's demo session and the songs J. D. and Willy hadn't finished yet. Meanwhile, Zeke and Alex huddled together in the corner, conspiring against David somehow, he was sure.

A functioning band, David understood, was really just a dysfunctional family.

J. D.: the Dependent, desperate for attention and threatening to bring the whole band down if he didn't get his way. But no one could call him out because he was the ideal lead singer—an incredible voice and pretty-boy looks—yet he was such a self-absorbed pain in the ass that David could barely stay in the same room with him.

Willy: the Enabler, rewriting lyrics J. D. didn't like,

changing keys so that J. D. could work in a wail that got the audience screaming. Willy was a great guitarist and song-writer, hands down the most talented member of the band, but Willy had hitched his star to J. D., and he was going to do whatever it took to keep J. D. happy.

So what did that make the rest of them? Alex: the Hero, playing killer guitar solos on stage and carrying equipment up three flights of stairs without complaining. Zeke: the Mascot, the goofy drummer with the heart of gold. And that left David, he realized, as something between the Scapegoat and the Lost Child, screwing up bass lines and moping around after shows while everyone else basked in being a band on the rise.

Then J. D. and Willy swept in with huge smiles on their faces and no plans to apologize for being 45 minutes late.

"This is it," J. D. shouted, holding up sheets of paper. "This is the music that's going to bust us out of this second-rate town. In my hands, I have our hit single. But, it's even more than that."

David hesitated briefly but then took the bait. "Why is it more than a hit single?"

J. D. smiled. He'd obviously been waiting for this. "Multiple revenue streams."

David didn't get it, though he recognized the term as one of those lines J. D. had picked up from a "make your fortune in real estate in just 30 days" DVD. J. D. had been a business major before dropping out of college, and he couldn't wait to spend the money the band hadn't earned yet.

J. D. continued. "It's the song we've been waiting for. It's called 'Invested in You.'"

By the way J. D. was beaming, David knew he was proud of himself, and the thing to do was to be as excited as J. D. was. Alex and Zeke were grinning supportively as though they had understood what J. D. meant, but David couldn't help but play the Scapegoat.

"J. D., that makes zero fucking sense. It's the stupidest song title I've ever heard."

That lit J. D.'s fuse, but before he could go off, Willy stepped up and stood right in front of David.

"Listen, check it out," Willy said, his voice sounding weary. His whole body looked tired with lanky limbs drooping from his torso. "This is my fourth band and the second time I've had a shot at a contract. And it's taken me this long to realize that a hit single is not enough. We keep talking like a contract with a label is going to save us, like a three-album deal is the end of the rainbow, but even if we become the next hot band, it won't matter. In ten years, we'll be lucky if anyone remembers our name. No matter how big our hit single is, there's hardly any money to be made from a song that's going to be stripped and down-loaded anywhere on the planet. The trick is to start with a hit single, come up with a song that's so goddamn catchy that people hum it when they try to go to sleep. Then we milk it: get the song in video games, on ringtones, on TV shows or movies. And, then we wait. When our fans get older and have more money, then we start selling the song for commercials. Think about it—'Invested in You'—every financial services company is going to want this to be their jingle. And after 'Invested in You,' we've got 'Built for Speed.' That one has lyrics the car companies are going to be dying for in twenty years."

When Willy finished, his hands were shaking. David could see everyone was waiting for him to accuse them of selling out. And David knew his role. Throw a fit, force the rest of the band to stand united against him, and then slink over to his amp with his tail between his legs. But he couldn't do it, even though he wanted to be disgusted with J. D. and Willy. He didn't want to keep playing gigs in the same dozen bars for the next decade. He wanted to be a rock star, even if being a rock star didn't mean as much anymore.

David cleared his throat. "Not 'Built for Speed.' That's the wrong title for the second song. It should be 'Built for Comfort.' In twenty years, our fans won't drive fast. They're going to want big, cushy cars for their big, cushy asses."

Willy smiled, and J. D. threw an arm around David's shoulder. The rest of the band approached, and for a second David thought there was going to be a family hug. Willy passed around the music for 'Invested in You.' David took a sheet and picked up his bass. He was ready to play.

Atmosphere

I'LL NEVER GET used to the space helmet. Three, maybe four times a day I try to scratch my nose or rub an itch on my lower left eye and, bam, I whack a hand right on the shell of the helmet. All three of my hands have bruises now. But since there's hardly any cyanide in the atmosphere, I'd be dead in seconds if I tried to breathe the oxygen on this planet. So, I'll have to put up with this helmet as long as we stay here on Earth, but I have to say I hope it won't be too long.

This planet has got to be the most inconvenient place in the universe. Half the day there's blinding light and then, when it gets dark, it's just dark. I mean, there's hardly any visible gas in the atmosphere, no chemical haze like there would be on a normal planet. And the days happen so fast that as soon as I have the visor on my helmet adjusted for the light, I have to readjust it for the dark.

It's stuff like that that drives me crazy about this planet. By the time I've finally gotten to really know one of the natives, she ups and dies and is replaced by her child or grandchild, and I'm like "Well, what the hell, why didn't anyone tell me the grandmother was dead?" and they say that it happened during one of my dormant cycles, like that's somehow my fault.

Apparently, my dormant cycles match up pretty close to this season they call "summer," where they all swear the weather is warmer and the foliage is more vibrant. They've even shown me pictures of this "summer," but the thing comes and goes so fast I don't have much faith in it. I'm supposed to be impressed by the fact that "summer" is hot, even though my planet has an average temperature variation of 500 degrees centigrade.

They keep thinking I'm going to be shocked by the height of their mountains or the strength of their storms. It's all I can do not to roll my eyes at them, well, at least my upper tier of eyes. These natives can't imagine the extremes of my home world. Volcanoes rise higher than can be seen. We have oceans larger than all of Earth. There are enormous creatures that only survive on my planet because they have symbiotic relationships with microscopic bacteria.

But I will say one thing. If I had to invent an atmosphere from scratch, I might go with oxygen, like they have here. Oh, I know what you're thinking. Cyanide is superior in so many ways. And, of course, that's true. But it's amazing how many different forms of life can breathe oxygen. I can't even keep track of them all. And even with all that the dominant species here is doing to eliminate rivals, the new life forms just keep coming. It's hard to explain how fast everything happens here. Civilizations rise and fall, species come into existence and go extinct, shifting tectonic plates rearrange the continents. Things are moving all the time. It's impossible to keep up with. At a certain point, you just have to give yourself up to the atmosphere and breathe it all in. So to speak.

Nativity Set

IT'S HARD WHEN we visit Beth's mother's house. At home, everything is baby proofed, taped down, or locked up, but when we visit we're always worried that our three-year-old, Katelyn, will spill a juice box on a white rug, or play with toxic cleaning chemicals under the kitchen sink, or break some family heirloom my mother-in-law insists on displaying on a low shelf.

So, one time, it was the morning of Christmas Eve, and it was my turn to get up with Katelyn (she gets up at 5:30 A.M., no matter when she goes to bed). We were in my mother-in-law's living room and Katelyn was playing quietly in a corner while I sat on a couch, dazed and semi-watching the same news reports on CNN for the third time. My mother-in-law came downstairs and headed over to give Katelyn a kiss good morning.

"Well, hello—ohh!" she gasped. "Katelyn, no!"

Something was wrong. From the tone of my mother-in-law's voice, it was my fault. I jumped up and saw Katelyn playing with my mother-in-law's imported porcelain nativity set, the family heirloom that was the centerpiece for Christmas dinner. It was the worst thing in the house for

Katelyn to touch, but there in the manger were the Virgin Mary and SpongeBob SquarePants gazing down on Baby Elmo in the crib. In the background stood two wise men and Dora the Explorer with camel figurines, an orange dinosaur, and most of a Barrel of Monkeys hanging from the rafters. It was a pretty clever scene, all in all, but I knew my role, particularly when my mother-in-law was watching. I sternly told Katelyn that though the nativity set did look like a dollhouse, it was not a toy. Then I put the set up on a bookshelf on the other side of the room.

Katelyn scowled at me and, in a perfect tone of annoyance and resignation, said, "Fucking A."

My jaw dropped and I glanced to my mother-in-law across the room, hoping she hadn't heard. I had to act fast.

"No, honey, your Fluffy May doll isn't down here. I think she's in the suitcase. Let's go look for Fluffy May."

I scooped up Katelyn and headed upstairs. My mother-in-law was rearranging the nativity set figurines and hadn't seemed to notice anything. When we got to the room where Katelyn slept, I put her on her bed and sat right next to her.

"Honey, that is not a nice thing to say. Where did you hear that?"

Katelyn said nothing.

"Katelyn, if you're mad, you should say, 'I'm mad at you.' Do you understand?"

She nodded back sweetly.

"I love you, Daddy."

"I love you, too, sweetheart."

The door opened and Beth came in, surprised to find the two of us on Katelyn's little bed.

"Well," Beth said, smiling, "this is a pretty scene."

"Hi, Mommy," Katelyn said brightly. "Fucking A."

Beth's smile disappeared. I explained what had happened in a way that showed that I wasn't to blame. Really, I was more of a "goddamnit" or "holy shit" kind of guy. I didn't think Katelyn had gotten "Fucking A" from me. I could tell Beth didn't believe me, but she was more worried about Katelyn swearing like that at church, never mind in front of her mom.

I agreed, but I didn't know what to do. If we made too big a deal out of it, Katelyn might just swear more. The thing to do was to ignore Katelyn and hope she moved on. But "Fucking A" was pretty hard to ignore.

Later that afternoon, Beth and her mom went shopping and I was keeping an eye on Katelyn. And I was, only I didn't notice when she must have climbed the bookshelf and taken down the nativity set figurines. I don't know how she did it without breaking any of them, but at halftime of the Bulls game when I turned off the set and checked on Katelyn, she had the nativity figurines and her tea set. Standing around tiny tables with little cups, saucers and teapots, were Joseph, a Disney princess, a shepherd, and a teddy bear missing an arm. Before them was a delicious snack of fake cookies and sheep.

I snatched up the pieces.

"Katelyn, these are not toys," I said, holding wise men.

Then I realized I also was holding her bendable Santa Claus doll, which looked like one of the wise men. "Except for Santa. He is a toy. Here."

I handed Santa back to Katelyn.

"Fucking A," she muttered.

I ignored her because we were the only ones in the house. And, to tell you the truth, it felt like a "Fucking A" moment.

Christmas came and we waded through an ocean of presents and the longest Christmas mass ever. Katelyn was on her best behavior, but I was on edge all day, expecting the outburst that would seal my fate as the bad-influence, indulgent parent that I really wasn't. Really.

For Christmas dinner, my mother-in-law cooked up a huge meal, even though there were only four of us (and one of us only ate macaroni and cheese). There was turkey, stuffing, mashed potatoes, four kinds of vegetables and two kinds of bread. The table was bursting except for an open spot in the center reserved for the nativity set. When we were all seated, my mother-in-law dimmed the lights and took the set from the bookshelf. She carefully made her way toward the table. Then, as we all watched, she stepped right on the singing Barney doll. As Barney burst into a round of "I Love You, You Love Me," my mother-in-law lost her footing and the nativity set crashed to the floor. Shepherds shattered, camels were decapitated, arms and legs of the Holy Family were tossed asunder.

We stared in shock and amazement as Barney finished

singing the chorus. Then my mother-in-law spoke:
    "Fucking A!"

My Future Career

I'M WRITING ABOUT my future career because that is the assignment for this class. I have to write five hundred words about this topic because that is what you said, Mrs. Keiler. You should know that this is a hard assignment because five hundred is a lot of words, and after I say I want to be a video game tester I won't have anything left to say and so far that's only seventy-five words.

Not everyone is good with words, especially when they have to be in the right order and in complete sentences and stuff. Teachers should think about that when they give out papers to write. In science class, I sit with Rebecca Mandal, who is always talking about her out-of-state boyfriend and texting him when she thinks nobody's looking. I'm sure for her five hundred words is like half a diary entry. But some people have to really work hard for words, and it's not fair for me to have to work harder than Rebecca.

I'm sure Rebecca is going to write about becoming a shoe designer after going to the college she's always talking about. I forget which one it is, but she already wears a sweatshirt with the college's name across the front. I suppose college is for some people, but I've got too much to do to spend four more years in school. You see, I know what I'm going to be when I grow up because I know what I'm great at, and it doesn't involve a lot of words: I'm going to be a video game tester. Somebody has to test all the new video games to make sure they work and that somebody is going to be me.

I am totally leet at Madden NFL and even found a disk glitch that you may know because I posted it on this really popular blog. You pause, go to substitutions, sub the back up center for the left guard, put the starting left guard in the center slot, then reset the subs when you run the formation. Pow! It's a total disconnect if you do it right. When I posted the glitch, this noob called me a griefer for ruining the game for him. I told the noob "get a brick and go back to playing sims. Oh, wait, you can't do that because you're a total high pinger." Ha! That was great. The noob didn't even bother posting back, but I got lots of "dittos" and a "GJP, boss man," and one gamer even said I should zap a line to the hot shots at Electronic Arts and get a job as a tester. That's when I knew what my future career would be once I get out of high school.

So now you know all about my future career. Being a video game tester means I won't have to work so hard at words because words can be really hard, but now I got exactly five hundred of them.

The Meta-Metamorphosis

As SAMANTHA BRIGGS awoke one morning from uneasy dreams, she found herself transformed in her bed into a gigantic insect. That's not very original, she thought, as she lay on her newly hard back staring at the various appendages sticking out from her new, vermin-like body.

She closed her eyes and wondered if she could just go back to sleep. She knew this story, after all, and it didn't end well.

However, Samantha found that she could not return to sleep. Instead, her thoughts went back to the previous night, and she tried to determine what could have brought about her transformation. She remembered being at the bar and drinking more than she knew at the time she should have. In fact, she drank enough that she used that hookup app she swore she would never use again.

But the app was flawless. Within minutes of swiping through a list of acceptable faces, one of them appeared by her side as if summoned by a magic spell, which was basically what had happened. He smiled eagerly, and his face was a little flushed as if he had just run over here to meet her, which was actually likely. He was tall and not quite as handsome as in his profile picture, but she had expected that. He bought her a drink, which was the last thing she needed, and struck up an aimless conversation, which she only needed slightly more. What she really desired was his enthusiasm and interest, and that he had been able to provide. His name, there must have been that as well.

Samantha opened her eyes again, in vain hope that her situation had changed. It had not. She was a bug.

What in the world was she going to do? She had a morning meeting at work, and she didn't even know what time it was. Samantha turned toward her nightstand, which was no mean feat in her condition. She had to use all the appendages on the left side of her insect body to prop herself up, so she could turn in that direction. Fortunately, the antenna that now grew out of her head was flexible enough that she could direct it toward her phone. She clumsily punched in her passcode and opened it. She had overslept and was already late for work.

It was hard for her eyes to focus on her phone's tiny screen, even though it now seemed as if she had more eyes than she had had the night before. She knew that after she had left the bar with that guy, they had stopped at a corner deli to get some food, and she tried to determine if she had checked in there or anywhere else for that matter. But her phone had nothing to tell her. Then she scrolled through her messages, wondering if she had texted that guy or made him a contact. But why would she have texted him? He had been with her all night. When had he left exactly?

She wasn't quite sure. Still, she gave the phone a look. After all, stranger things had happened.

Take, for example, the fact that she was still an insect. She tried to sit up in bed, but found that she had no abdominal muscles and could not sit. Instead, she leaned even further toward the end table, forcing her many appendages to strain against the mattress. But she didn't know the strength of her insect body, because she flung herself off the bed and into her end table sending her phone and lamp clattering to the ground as she landed with a thud on the hard, cold floor.

If she had had a roommate, the noise would have brought her running. But Samantha lived alone, had lived alone since she had gotten her first full-time job. She told herself she preferred it that way, not having to worry about someone else, not having to meet anyone else's expectations. She did believe these things, but there were more nights than she wished to admit, nights when she had streamed every movie worth streaming, when she wouldn't have minded having a roommate.

If she had had a roommate now, she would have called to the roommate for help because her side began to throb where she had collided with the end table. One of her many legs was tangled in the sheets on the edge of her bed, and her phone had slid under the dresser out of reach. Though there was no one to hear her, Samantha called out anyway. Her voice didn't sound human. It was a cross between a screech and a skitter. For the first time Samantha was truly scared.

Then her phone started to buzz. Was it someone from work who was looking for her or maybe the guy from last night? Perhaps it was the roommate she never had, calling to just see how she was feeling.

She would have liked to tell the roommate she never had that she was not feeling well, but the phone was out of reach and the more she tried to move her insect body toward it, the more she became twisted in the sheets at the edge of her bed.

The phone stopped buzzing. The entire apartment was quiet except for the slow wheeze of air in and out of what had been Samantha's mouth. She would miss her morning meeting, of that she was sure. Of what else was in store for her, now and perhaps forever, she had no idea.

A Simple Realization

My REVELATION came in the middle of a blizzard. It had been snowing for eighteen straight hours. Streets were closed, power lines were down, we were trapped in our apartment, and Sara, at the time my wife of six months, had just thrown a plate at my head. Fortunately she missed and the plate shattered against the kitchen wall. As I swept the shards off the floor, watching the snow silently accumulate and listening to Sara's muffled cries from the bedroom, I had my revelation. This is what I realized: marriages weren't supposed to last. At least for me, that is.

This was a simple realization, perhaps, but it allowed me to view everything differently. My two previous marriages hadn't "failed," their time had just come to an end. There needed to be an expiration date stamped on my marriage licenses. I decided then and there to change my ways. From then on I would avoid heated conversations, forget about counseling, and just take the inevitable collapse in stride. It was like bringing out the big parka for the coldest days of winter. You just kept yourself warm, knowing that the season would change eventually.

I could now see that things between Sara and me had

fallen into a familiar pattern. Sure, it started off with home-cooked meals, exciting vacations, and a mutual understanding about the need for personal space. But soon enough it was fast food, television reruns, and tossed china during arguments over "responsibility." I was tired of sweeping up the glass.

I suppose a more cynical man would have turned his back on marriage altogether. But why should my wives and I have been deprived of all the great times early on? What was the point of missing out on the good things in life just because they didn't last? My divorce from Sara ended up being the easiest of my three to date, and I didn't forget the lessons I had learned.

Kim, my next wife, was quite a few years younger than I was. I could have made myself miserable trying to keep up with her. But now that I didn't expect the marriage to last, I was able to enjoy my time with Kim on my terms. She wasn't quite as understanding as my other wives, but I had learned to accept that too.

Then there was Terry or was it Tina? I can never remember who came next. But since neither marriage lasted that long, it doesn't really matter. But Olivia, ah, she was the one who got away. For her, who knows, I might have betrayed my principles. But she didn't stick around to give me that chance.

Now that I'm nearing retirement, I find I'm losing interest in the chase. I just don't have the patience for all that's involved with meeting, dating, and marrying. Rebecca, my current wife, might be my last go-round. Maybe I'll be able to stretch this one out, as we've been happy together in surprising ways so far. Rebecca never had children of her own, so she's really relished the role of stepmother. She keeps tabs on all the kids and remembers their birthdays. Rebecca's really something; I have a hard time just keeping all the names straight, but she's now convinced some of them to even start coming around for holidays. And I find that I enjoy the kids more now too, as long as they're not trying to get college tuition out of me, that is. So, we'll see how things play out. I'd really like to do more travelling after I retire, see more of the world. Anything to avoid falling into a routine. Routine is just the death of you.

The Answer

THE NOTE SAID, "Look to the mirror for the answer." I didn't have to be a detective to find the mirror, a gaudy, gothic-looking mistake taking up most of the back wall. The front of the room opened onto a balcony looking over white cliffs and crashing surf. It could have been a beautiful space, but the animal heads mounted throughout the room ruined everything. And the blood. That didn't help. I stared again at the mirror, seeing only my reflection and the open French doors behind me. I didn't know why there was a corpse lying at my feet.

Meeting

WHEN THE MEETING had passed the one-hour mark and they were still discussing "Potential Software Upgrade," which was only item two out of seven on the agenda, Philip began making lists in his head. The first list was simple enough: Things To Pick Up On The Way Home: skim milk, whole wheat bread, maybe eggs, one of those shiny things that fits on the end of the garden hose, and a purple-but-not-too-purple three-ring binder.

Then he worked on Things To Do This Weekend: fix the leak in the upstairs sink, mow the lawn, watch the season of *Mad Men* that he'd recorded on the DVR, and finish reading the biography of James K. Polk The Polk biography was part of Philip's long-term goal of reading biographies of all the presidents in the order that they served. He had made great progress through the Founding Fathers but had bogged down ever since Martin Van Buren, and he was trying to avoid the temptation to skip ahead to the Civil War.

As the meeting continued, Philip couldn't tell whether they were still discussing item two, "Potential Software Upgrade," or if they had moved on to item three, "Support Staffing Challenges." He started a list he called People I Hate. At the top of the list was Charles, his immediate supervisor, the one who was so mishandling this meeting that conversation had inexplicably circled back to the first agenda item ("Ideas for Cost Savings"). The People I Hate list also included Steve Bridgeman, who was sitting across the table from him dutifully writing down unworkable cost savings ideas such as "totally paperless office," "use Skype to replace all overseas travel," and "eliminate employee parking lot." Philip then added the name of his high school art teacher, Mrs. Maples, to the list. How could you not hate someone who gave you detention because she thought your sculpture of the Washington Monument was a penis? Of course, the list also had to include Tim Williams, the obnoxious, drum-playing former roommate who had left town without paying rent and cost Philip his security deposit at a time in his life when he had already been subsisting on Ramen noodles and hors d'oeuvres poached from openings at art galleries.

Philip realized the People I Hate list wasn't improving his mood, and neither was the fact that the meeting had suddenly skipped ahead to the fifth agenda item, "Reflections on Loss of CynaDyme Account," so he started a People I Love list. Sarah, Philip's wife, remained at the top of that list, where she had been since he met her at an art opening he had only gone to for the free food. At the time, since Sarah's paintings were on display and she was wearing this amazing dress, he assumed she had had it all together. It was only after they started dating that he discovered she was living as close to the edge as he was back then. But Sarah wasn't the type to worry. It was part of what drew Philip to her. Even in those years right after Melody was born when neither of them had full-time work, Sarah stayed serene, and somehow that convinced Philip that things would work out. It was still incredible to him that they were both now living like real adults, with regular jobs and a house. And Sarah was still as creative and unpredictable as she had been when they first met, only now they lived in the most colorfully painted home in the neighborhood.

Their daughter, Melody, was right at the top of the People I Love list as well, even though she currently was in a phase marked by dramatic sighs and eye rolling whenever Philip offered suggestions as to what Melody should be watching on TV or how she might put her clothes in a drawer rather than on her floor so that she wouldn't have to walk through a trench just to get to her bed. But just last night, when he had fallen asleep in the living room, midway through a mind-numbing chapter on James K. Polk's creation of the Department of the Interior, he was aware that Melody had taken the book out of his hands and placed a bookmark in it before setting it down on the coffee table.

And, Philip had to admit, his brother Jacob was on the People I Love list. Jacob hadn't always been on that list, especially during those bad years lost to drugs when he stole money from Philip and alienated everyone around him. But Jacob had gotten his act together, and even though he was still sleeping on a couch in Philip's basement, he had been able to hold down a steady job for the first time in years. There were some nights when they'd meet out in the backyard at the basketball hoop Philip had set up, and for brief moments—usually after sinking a three-pointer under pressure—it seemed to Philip like they were still kids, playing around at home in the twilight after dinner, lofting shot after shot until it got too dark to see the hoop clearly, and he'd hear his mom calling him to come inside, "Philip, Philip."

"Philip. Philip. You still with us?" It was Charles, his boss. Across the table, Steve Bridgeman had a smirk on his face.

"Yes, sorry, Charles."

"So, will you be able to take care of that for next week?"

"Yes, absolutely. I've got it right here. On my list."

Just Hands

Scene: ARTIST and AGENT in conversation. Automatically rotating slideshow of pictures of hands playing behind them.

AGENT

Is that it?

ARTIST

What do you mean, "Is that it?" Of course, that's it. Don't you like it?

AGENT

Of course I like it. I really do. I mean, it's really something. It's just . . .

ARTIST

It's just what?

AGENT

It's just . . . well, is it all just hands?

ARTIST

(*slightly exasperated*) Yes, it's all just hands. Is there something wrong with that?

AGENT

Oh no, not at all. I mean, I get it. It's great. It's just that I guess I wasn't expecting it to be all hands.

ARTIST

Well, I don't know why that should be a surprise. The project is called "Hands."

AGENT

Yes, yes, I understand. But, you know, you've been working on this project for a while, and you got that big grant, so I just thought this would be different. I mean, these pictures don't look like your style. It doesn't even look like you took them.

ARTIST

What are you talking about? Of course, I didn't take them.

AGENT

You didn't? Well, I guess I am confused then. Where did all these hands come from?

ARTIST

People sent them to me. You know, texting and Twitter. It's

unbelievable how many different hands there are. (*pauses, stares at images of hands*). Wow, I guess I'm really going to have to spend a lot of time writing my artist statement. You don't like it, do you?

AGENT

It's not that I don't like it. I guess it's just not what I was expecting, you know? It's like, let's say I had written a book of stories and you were reading it and all the stories turned out to be really short. You know what I mean?

ARTIST

No, I have no idea what you mean.

AGENT

Well then, take your last project. You took all those pictures with the large format camera, and they were printed on that high gloss paper. Now, that really made an impression. I mean, that stood out. But this... and I like it, don't get me wrong, but I kind of feel like I could see this anywhere.

ARTIST

(*becoming agitated*) But don't you see? That's the whole point. You can see this anywhere. All around you. Hands, everywhere. But when have you looked at them? When have you stopped to look at all the hands, all the different fingers, the rings, the manicures and the scars? Have you ever really stopped and asked to see someone's hand?

AGENT

Hey, calm down. I get it. I get it.

ARTIST

No, you don't get it. Have you ever done that? Have you ever asked to see someone's hand?

AGENT

Come on, if I was in a room full of people and I asked to see someone's hands, I'd probably get arrested, but I've got nothing against hands. Hands are great.

ARTIST

(*puts hands behind back*) Really? What can you tell me about mine?

AGENT

Don't be silly.

ARTIST

No, I mean it. What can you tell me, beyond ten fingers and two palms?

AGENT

I, well . . . okay, you're right . . . I can't. I can't tell you any-thing. I've known you for almost fifteen years, and I've sold dozens of your photographs, but I can't tell you anything about your hands.

ARTIST

Thank you. That's all I wanted to hear.

(*Pause. Both look at hands on screen.*)

AGENT

Well, I'll see what I can do. It sure is a lot of hands.

ARTIST

Yeah. There are a lot of hands out there.

Google Autocomplete Suggestions for "Why"

WHY IS THE SKY BLUE? Why is gluten bad? Why is the ocean salty? Why is Ziva leaving *NCIS*? Why am I so tired? Why do we yawn? Why is my period late? Why is my period early? Why is my internet so slow? Why is my pool cloudy? Why is my poop green? Why is my eye twitching? Why is *The Heat* rated R? Why is *The Call* rated R? Why is T*he Purge* rated R? Why is the thumb not a finger? Why is the theory of evolution not a law? Why is the thunder so loud? Why is Amanda Bynes crazy? Why is a tomato a fruit? Why is A-Rod still playing? Why is an atom electrically neutral? Why is a manhole cover round? Why is our planet called Earth? Why is our blood red? Why is there fuzz on a tennis ball? Why is there a civil war in Syria? Why is there an ammo shortage? Why is there a helium shortage? Why is there blood in my urine? Why is there a leap year? Why is Amber Rose bald? Why is a dollar called a buck? Why is the rum gone? Why is the rum always gone?

Dean Dean Dean Dean

A flash serial in four parts

Dean

HE WAS BORN Jimmy Dean, named after his maternal grandfather, James, or so he thought. And though that name brought little joy—the boys in his preschool had teased little Jimmy and called him "sausage man"—he still had come to think of it as his own.

But when Jimmy entered kindergarten and his birth certificate was needed for registration, it was discovered that his first name was not Jimmy but Dean. In fact, his full name was nothing but Deans: Dean Dean Dean, right there on the paper. When his mother confronted his father with this slip of paper, a piece of parchment that shook as her hand quivered, his father puffed up in anger and righteousness. His father was a blues rock guitarist known for both fiery solos and alcohol-fueled tirades, so he did anger and righteousness well.

"What's wrong with my family name?" his father retorted. "Dean is a fine name. I wasn't going to name my son after a man who hates me."

In fact, his mother's whole side of the family hated his father, and at this low moment in their marriage, his mother could see their point. She took Jimmy, now Dean, and left his father, moving back to her hometown.

This new arrangement made his mother happy—after a quick divorce she married her high school sweetheart, the manager of a local fast food restaurant known for the crispness of its French fries—but it was a difficult transition for Dean, primarily because he didn't know who he was. When a teacher called out "Dean," he would turn his head to look for someone else. And the kids at his new school were suspicious of a boy with one name used three times. It seemed to them an elaborate ruse to use repetition to get higher marks in penmanship.

The kids were right, in a way. To get used to the idea of being Dean, he would write "Dean" over and over again in a notebook, in careful looping cursive. But after writing the name on page after page, it didn't seem any more his own. The letters seemed to lose meaning the more he wrote them, and he started to see them as shapes more than signs. He still didn't know who he was, but, damn, did he have nice handwriting!

Dean Dean

As a teenager, Dean Dean listened to music on the radio all the time, except he didn't really listen to the music. What Dean Dean was really interested in was radio DJs, or, to be more specific, those instances when DJs segued from one song to another. He became obsessed with such moments of transition, carefully using a notebook to document shifts such as the change from the Police's "Every Little Thing She Does Is Magic" to Journey's "Open Arms."

Dean Dean's father saw this interest as just another sign of all that had gone wrong since the 1970s had become the 1980s. By now, his father's music career consisted of little more than regrets, a fact that his father hadn't fully accepted. His father also hadn't fully accepted the fact that Dean Dean's mother had divorced him and remarried. Because of his father's refusal to accept changes he had not acquiesced to, Dean Dean saw more of him than might otherwise have been the case.

"I should have never let you quit taking guitar lessons," his father would rant. "Then maybe there'd be one teenager left in the USA who appreciated good music."

Dean Dean wouldn't contradict his father, but it had been his father who insisted that Dean Dean stop playing guitar when it became clear that Dean Dean had little interest in the instrument and would only practice when forced to. Dean Dean had been glad to stop the lessons, which he had only started in the first place at his father's insistence. But the lessons weren't a complete waste of time. Dean Dean developed a good enough ear to realize that "Every Little Thing She Does Is Magic" and "Open Arms" were both in D major, an insight that he made sure to write down in his notebook.

Dean Dean's mother was concerned about his obsession. She would have liked to see him leave his bedroom more often, and she worried that he didn't really seem to have friends. However, his obsessive nature made him an attentive student. Dean Dean got good grades and became the first person in his family to go to college. He became a sound engineer at the college's radio station, which allowed him to control sound without having to make any himself. He kept to himself and never had a wide circle of friends, but he did excel in the classroom, where he was particularly good at doing what he was told. His professors told him to keep it up, so he did, continuing on to graduate school. Later, when a university hired him as a sound engineer/instructor in a Department of Film, TV, and Radio, Dean Dean thought that maybe that was who he was.

Dean Dean Dean

THE ONLY PROBLEM for Dean Dean Dean was that being an instructor required him to teach. That meant he had to stand in front of a class with people looking at him, expecting him to talk. All of this was terrifying, and none of it went well. He dreaded going into the classroom each morning, and he feared his students dreaded it even more. To ease his anxiety, he began playing music in class, demonstrating various modes of transition from song to song, which was highly irregular in a course titled "Marconi and the History of Early Radio."

"You hear that? When a song ends cold, like Talking Heads' "And She Was," you have to be ready to switch right away to the next song. In fact, because it takes about half a rotation for a turntable to get to the right speed, if you don't want dead air, you have to begin the next song in the split second before the previous song has ended."

"Excuse me," a student in the front row interrupted. "I don't see what this has to do with the history of early radio."

Dean Dean Dean narrowed his gaze at the student. It was a quizzical look, but it must have seemed withering, because when Dean Dean Dean continued talking, the student stayed silent.

"Of course, it is more common for a song to gradually fade out, which makes for a smoother transition. The best segues not only seamlessly move from one song to another but also connect up musically. Segueing between two songs in the same key will sound natural, as will segues between songs that are in harmonically related keys."

Dean Dean Dean found it uncomfortable to look at students when he spoke, so he stared at the two turntables on the desk in front of him.

"Now, some bands realize the importance of segues, and it's not uncommon for album-oriented rock to incorporate segues into the production. You can hear this as early back as the second side of the Beatles' *Sgt. Pepper's* album. Or take Pink Floyd's *The Dark Side of the Moon*. All the songs on that album segue into one another, as if it is one continuous medley."

"Hey, Professor!" a voice rang out from the back of the room. It came from a boy wearing a baseball cap backwards. "Since you have two turntables, can you do some scratching?"

Dean Dean Dean looked at the boy in horror. He understood scratching as a concept, but he could not imagine why anyone would so defile a piece of vinyl. He continued on.

"But perhaps the most significant segues happen when two songs can be made to speak to one another thematically or lyrically. What's the proper response to "I Want To Know What Love Is," that maudlin and overproduced Foreigner song?" Here, despite himself, he paused and looked at the class for an answer. There was none.

"J. Geils Band's 'Love Stinks,' of course."

Another hand went up. It was a student Dean Dean Dean had noticed before because of her copious note taking and careful handwriting. He nodded toward her hopefully.

In a quiet, hesitant tone, she spoke. "Do you have any examples involving music we know?"

Dean Dean Dean Dean

THERE WERE OTHER problems. Having an instructor named Dean Dean Dean was more than the University's webpage could handle. When anyone searched for information on the University, Dean Dean Dean's name came up again and again and again. It was as if all those Deans were so insistent that they pushed their way to the top of the results page.

The issue itself had become so troubling that it rose to the top of the agenda at the highest levels of the University. A meeting was called between various Deans, the Provost, the Vice Provost, and the Vice Vice Provost. The University's webmaster had also been invited to the meeting, but he refused to attend over an ongoing dispute as to whether his job title could be officially changed to "Web Guru."

"Can't we do something about Instructor Dean?" asked the Dean of the Engineering College.

"We're trying," said the Vice Provost, "but until we resolve this whole 'web guru' issue, no one can make any changes to our website."

"Can't we just fire the webmaster?" pleaded the Nursing School Dean.

"We did already," said the Vice Vice Provost, "but we had to hire him back as a consultant because he's the only person who can update the website."

"Hang on," the Provost interrupted. "The Vice Vice Vice Provost is in charge of the website. Where is she?"

"She's in the hospital," the Vice Provost replied. "She was walking into her office when the new Vice Vice Vice Provost nameplate fell off the top of the door and knocked her unconscious."

"I should have seen it coming," the Provost said, shaking his head. "Too many Vices."

"Can't we do something?" the Engineering College Dean said again, banging his fist on the conference table.

Everyone paused. This was a breach of etiquette from a man no one liked anyway. But no one had an answer for him either, and the meeting ended in dissatisfaction.

It seemed as if there was no answer to the problem of Dean Dean Dean. Then, just when things seemed hopeless, events took a turn for the better when the Engineering School Dean was hit by a bus and killed. This created an opening for a new Dean.

Another meeting was called, and this time the Vice Vice Vice Provost, who had been released from the hospital, was able to attend. "Are you sure we can make an instructor the Dean of the Engineering School?" the Vice Vice Vice Provost asked, her voice muffled by bandages.

"Of course we can," the Provost insisted. "He's an engineer, isn't he?"

"Well," the Vice Vice Vice Provost continued, ignoring the throbbing pain in the side of her head, "he's a sound engineer in the Department of Film, TV, and Radio."

"What?" the Provost exclaimed. "We have a Department of Film, TV, and Radio? Do they not know there's an internet now? Whose idea was that department?"

An awkward silence followed, which the Provost correctly interpreted to mean that the idea had, in fact, been his.

It was time for the Provost to take bold action, particularly when the bold and the obvious intersected to look partly like a Venn diagram and partly like a delicious pastry. Besides, it was almost time for lunch, and the Provost was getting hungry.

And so Jimmy Dean became Dean Dean Dean Dean, but you might not know that because you've probably never seen him. Almost no one has. He refuses to meet with anyone. Rumor has it though that if you put your ear to his office door and listen carefully, you can hear the sound of songs transitioning from one to the next, over and over again.

I've Been Asked to Make
a Few Announcements

BEFORE WE GET started, I've been asked to make a few announcements. First, if you brought any food with you, please make sure not to leave it behind. Apparently, there was an incident here a little while ago. It may or may not have involved a rodent. I didn't ask. Just make sure to take all your food with you.

Then, there's a car in the parking lot with its lights on. It's a blue Ford with a dent on the right rear bumper. Not a big dent, just one of those little divots that could happen if you weren't paying attention while backing out of a parking space at the supermarket, maybe thinking about how you were already running late and still had to make dinner. Wondering how secure your job really was, because so many things that seemed so sure such a short time ago now seemed uncertain. Anyway, your lights are on.

Also, someone has lost a jacket. It's a light brown, almost rust-colored coat, with worn sleeves around the elbow and a frayed collar. It could be that the jacket was left behind intentionally, that it had been worn long enough, but its owner felt that it had some utility left in it and was hoping that someone else would take it, hoping that someone else would find a measure of use or pleasure in its wearing. It does appear to be a well cared for jacket, as if it had been packed away carefully for the winter and brought out again in the spring for when the wind was just a bit crisp. You can pick up that jacket on the way out if it's yours.

If there's a Sarah Powers here, your roommate has just called. You apparently left your cell phone at the apartment, and while this could have been intentional—after all, not everyone needs to be reachable at every moment—still, you may have wanted to have it with you. It's not so much that you're expecting anyone to call, but sometimes you like to have the phone during what you think of as the "moments between moments," the walk across a big parking lot, or the wait in a long check-out line, or when you simply feel lonely and don't know when the next good time will happen. At those moments between moments it's good to have the phone, to be able to call someone just to reassure yourself that you're not alone, that there are people who are interested in you and would be concerned if you just holed up in your room and refused to come out. So, Sarah, please get in touch with your roommate.

Finally, please take note of the emergency exits in this room in the unlikely event that we are forced to evacuate. It's good to be aware of what could occur even though we all know that you can't live your life expecting that the worst possible thing is going to happen. After all, if you did that you never would come out of your room, and here you are tonight. So that says something.

JIM O'LOUGHLIN is an associate professor of English at the University of Northern Iowa, where he teaches courses in American literature, creative writing and digital humanities. He is the director of the long-running Final Thursday Reading Series and Final Thursday Press. He lives in Cedar Falls, Iowa, with his wife and children. *Dean Dean Dean Dean* is his first collection.